MORE THAN A COMPANION: A REGENCY ROMANCE

LADIES ON THEIR OWN: GOVERNESSES AND COMPANIONS (BOOK 1)

ROSE PEARSON

MORE THAN A COMPANION

Ladies on their Own: Governesses and Companions

(Book 1)

By

Rose Pearson

© Copyright 2022 by Rose Pearson - All rights reserved.

In no way is it legal to reproduce, duplicate, or transmit any part of this document by either electronic means or in printed format. Recording of this publication is strictly prohibited and any storage of this document is not allowed unless with written permission from the publisher. All rights reserved.

Respective author owns all copyrights not held by the publisher.

MORE THAN A COMPANION

PROLOGUE

"Did you hear me, Honora?"

Miss Honora Gregory lifted her head at once, knowing that her father did not refer to her as 'Honora' very often and that he only did so when he was either irritated or angry with her.

"I do apologize, father, I was lost in my book," Honora replied, choosing to be truthful with her father rather than make excuses, despite the ire she feared would now follow. "Forgive my lack of consideration."

This seemed to soften Lord Greene just a little, for his scowl faded and his lips were no longer taut.

"I shall only repeat myself the once," her father said firmly, although there was no longer that hint of frustration in his voice. "There is very little money, Nora. I cannot give you a Season."

All thought of her book fled from Honora's mind as her eyes fixed to her father's, her chest suddenly tight. She had known that her father was struggling financially, although she had never been permitted to be aware of the details. But not to have a Season was deeply upsetting, and Honora had to immediately fight back hot tears which sprang into her eyes. There had always been a little hope in her heart, had always been a flicker of expectation that, despite knowing her father's situation, he might still be able to take her to London."

"Your aunt, however, is eager to go to London," Lord Greene continued, as Honora pressed one hand to her stomach in an attempt to soothe the sudden rolling and writhing which had captured her. He waved a hand dismissively, his expression twisting. "I do not know the reasons for it, given that she is widowed and, despite that, happily settled, but it seems she is determined to have some time in London this summer. Therefore, whilst you are not to have a Season of your own – you will not be presented or the like – you will go with your aunt to London."

Honora swallowed against the tightness in her throat, her hands twisting at her gown as she fought against a myriad of emotions.

"I am to be her companion?" she said, her voice only just a whisper as her father nodded.

She had always been aware that Lady Langdon, her aunt, had only ever considered her own happiness and her own situation, but to invite your niece to London as your companion rather than chaperone her for a Season surely spoke of selfishness!

"It is not what you might have hoped for, I know," her father continued, sounding resigned as a small sigh escaped his lips, his shoulders slumping. Honora looked up at him, seeing him now a little grey and realizing the full extent of his weariness. Some of her upset faded as she took in her father's demeanor, knowing that his lack of financial security was not his doing. The estate lands had done poorly these last three years, what with drought one year and flooding the next. As such, money had been ploughed into the ground to restore it and yet it would not become profitable again for at least another year. She could not blame her father for that. And yet, her heart had struggled against such news, trying to be glad that she would be in London but broken-hearted to learn that her aunt wanted her as her companion and nothing more. "I will not join you, of course," Lord Greene continued, coming a little closer to Honora and tilting his head just a fraction, studying his daughter carefully and, perhaps, all too aware of her inner turmoil. "You can, of course, choose to refuse your aunt's invitation – but I can offer you nothing more than what is being given to you at present, Nora. This may be your only opportunity to be in London."

Honora blinked rapidly against the sudden flow of hot tears that threatened to pour from her eyes, should she permit them.

"It is very good of my aunt," she managed to say, trying to be both gracious and thankful whilst ignoring the other, more negative feelings which troubled her. "Of course, I shall go."

Lord Greene smiled sadly, then reached out and settled one hand on Honora's shoulder, bending down just a little as he did so.

"My dear girl, would that I could give you more. You already have enough to endure, with the loss of your mother when you were just a child yourself. And now you have a poor father who cannot provide for you as he ought."

"I understand, Father," Honora replied quickly, not wanting to have her father's soul laden with guilt. "Pray, do not concern yourself. I shall be contented enough with what Lady Langdon has offered me."

Her father closed his eyes and let out another long sigh, accompanied this time with a shake of his head.

"She may be willing to allow you a little freedom, my dear girl," he said, without even the faintest trace of hope in his voice. "My sister has always been inclined to think only of herself, but there may yet be a change in her character."

Honora was still trying to accept the news that she was to be a companion to her aunt and could not make even a murmur of agreement. She closed her eyes, seeing a vision of herself standing in a ballroom, surrounded by ladies and gentlemen of the *ton*. She could almost hear the music, could almost feel the warmth on her skin... and then realized that she would be sitting quietly at the back of the room, able only to watch, and not to engage with any of it. Pain etched itself across her heart and Honora let out a long, slow breath, allowing the news to sink into her very soul.

"Thank you, Father." Her voice was hoarse but her words heartfelt, knowing that her father was doing his very best for her in the circumstances. "I will be a good companion for my aunt."

"I am sure that you will be, my dear," he said, quietly. "And I will pray that, despite everything, you might find a match – even in the difficulties that face us."

The smile faded from Honora's lips as, with that, her father left the room. There was very little chance of such a thing happening, as she was to be a companion rather than a debutante. The realization that she would be an afterthought, a lady worth nothing more than a mere glance from the moment that she set foot in London, began to tear away at Honora's heart, making her brow furrow and her lips pull downwards. There could be no moments of sheer enjoyment for her, no time when she was not considering all that was required of her as her aunt's companion. She would have to make certain that her thoughts were always fixed on her responsibilities, that her intentions were settled on her aunt at all times. Yes, there would be gentlemen to smile at and, on the rare chance, mayhap even converse with, but her aunt would not often permit such a thing, she was sure. Lady Langdon had her own reasons for going to London for the Season, whatever they were, and Honora was certain she would take every moment for herself.

"I must be grateful," Honora murmured to herself, setting aside her book completely as she rose from her chair and meandered towards the window.

Looking out at the grounds below, she took in the gardens, the pond to her right and the rose garden to her left. There were so many things here that held such beauty and, with it, such fond memories that there was a part of her, Honora had to admit, which did not want to leave it, did not want to set foot in London where she might find herself in a new and lower situation. There was security here, a comfort which encouraged her to remain, which told her to hold fast to all that she knew – but Honora was all too aware that she could not. Her future was not here. When her father passed away, if she was not wed, then Honora knew that she would be left to continue on as a companion, just to make certain that she had a home and enough coin for her later years. That was not the future she wanted but, she considered, it might very well be all that she could gain. Tears began to swell in her eyes, and she dropped her head, squeezing her eyes closed and forcing the tears back. This was the only opportunity she would have to go to London and, whilst it was not what she had hoped for, Honora had to accept it for what it was and begin to prepare herself for leaving her father's house – possibly, she considered, for good. Clasping both hands together, Honora drew in a long breath and let it out slowly as her eyes closed and her shoulders dropped.

A new part of her life was beginning. A new and unexpected future was being offered to her, and Honora had no other choice but to grasp it with both hands.

CHAPTER ONE

*P*ushing all doubt aside, Robert walked into White's with the air of someone who expected not only to be noticed, but to be greeted and exclaimed over in the most exaggerated manner. His chin lifted as he snapped his fingers towards one of the waiting footmen, giving him his request for the finest of brandies in short, sharp words. Then, he continued to make his way inside, his hands swinging loosely by his sides, his shoulders pulled back and his chest a little puffed out.

"Goodness, is that you?"

Robert grinned, his expectations seeming to be met, as a gentleman to his left rose to his feet and came towards him, only for him to stop suddenly and shake his head.

"Forgive me, you are not Lord Johnstone," he said, holding up both hands, palms out, towards Robert. "I thought that you were he, for you have a very similar appearance."

Grimacing, Robert shrugged and said not a word, making his way past the gentleman and finding a slight heat rising into his face. To be mistaken for another was one thing, but to remain entirely unrecognized was quite another! His doubts attempted to come rushing back. Surely someone would remember him, would remember what he had done last Season?

"Lord Crampton, good evening."

Much to his relief, Robert heard his title being spoken and turned his head to the right, seeing a gentleman sitting in a high-backed chair, a glass of brandy in his hand and a small smile on his face as he looked up at Robert.

"Good evening, Lord Marchmont," Robert replied, glad indeed that someone, at least, had recognized him. "I am back in London, as you can see."

"I hope you find it a pleasant visit," came the reply, only for Lord Marchmont to turn away and continue speaking to another gentleman sitting opposite – a man whom Robert had neither seen, nor was acquainted with. There was no suggestion from Lord Marchmont about introducing Robert to him and, irritated, Robert turned sharply away. His head dropped, his shoulders rounded, and he did not even attempt to keep his frustration out of his expression. His jaw tightened, his eyes blazed and his hands balled into fists.

Had they all forgotten him so quickly?

Practically flinging himself into a large, overstuffed armchair in the corner of White's, Robert began to mutter darkly to himself, almost angry about how he had been treated. Last Season he had been the talk of London! Why should he be so easily forgotten now? Unpleasant memories rose, of being inconspicuous, and disregarded, when he had first inherited his title. He attempted to push them aside, but his upset grew steadily so that even the brandy he was given by the footman – who had spent some minutes trying to find Lord Crampton – tasted like ash in his mouth. Nothing took his upset away and Robert wrapped it around his shoulders like a blanket, huddling against it and keeping it close to him.

He had not expected this. He had hoped to be not only remembered but celebrated! When he stepped into a room, he thought that he should be noticed. He *wanted* his name to be murmured by others, for it to be spread around the room that he had arrived! Instead, he was left with an almost painful frustration that he had been so quickly forgotten by the *ton* who, only a few months ago, had been his adoring admirers.

"Another brandy might help remove that look from your face." Robert did not so much as blink, hearing the man's voice but barely acknowledging it. "You are upset, I can tell." The man rose and came to sit opposite Robert, who finally was forced to recognize him. "That is no way for a gentleman to appear upon his first few days in London!"

Robert's lip curled. He should not, he knew, express his frustration so openly, but he found that he could not help himself.

"Good evening, Lord Burnley," he muttered, finding the man's broad smile and bright eyes to be nothing more than an irritation. "Are *you* enjoying the London Season thus far?"

Lord Burnley chuckled, his eyes dancing - which added to Robert's irritation all the more. He wanted to turn his head away, to make it plain to Lord Burnley that he did not enjoy his company and wanted very much to be free of it, but his standing as a gentleman would not permit him to do so.

"I have only been here a sennight but yes, I have found a great deal of enjoyment thus far," Lord Burnley told him. "But you should expect that, should you not? After all, a gentleman coming to London for the Season comes for good company, fine wine, excellent conversation and to be in the company of beautiful young ladies – one of whom might even catch his eye!"

This was, of course, suggestive of the fact that Lord Burnley might have had his head turned already by one of the young women making their come out, but Robert was in no mood to enter such a discussion. Instead, he merely sighed, picked up his glass again and held it out to the nearby footman, who came over to them at once.

"Another," he grunted, as the man took his glass from him. "And for Lord Burnley here."

Lord Burnley chuckled again, the sound grating on Robert's skin.

"I am quite contented with what I have at present, although I thank you for your consideration," he replied, making Robert's brow lift in surprise. What sort of gentleman turned down the opportunity to drink fine brandy? Half wishing that Lord Burnley would take his leave so that he might sit here in silence and roll around in his frustration, Robert settled back in his chair, his arms crossed over his chest and his gaze turned away from Lord Burnley in the vain hope that this would encourage the man to take his leave. He realized that he was behaving churlishly, yet somehow, he could not prevent it – he had hoped so much, and so far, nothing was as he had expected. "So, you are returned to London," Lord Burnley said, making Robert roll his eyes at the ridiculous observation which, for whatever reason, Lord Burnley either did not notice or chose to ignore. "Do you have any particular intentions for this Season?"

Sending a lazy glance towards Lord Burnley, Robert shrugged.

"If you mean to ask whether or not I intend to pursue

one particular young lady with the thought of matrimony in mind, then I must tell you that you are mistaken to even *think* that I should care for such a thing," he stated, plainly. "I am here only to enjoy myself."

"I see."

Lord Burnley gave no comment in judgment of Robert's statement, but Robert felt it nonetheless, quite certain that Lord Burnley now thought less of him for being here solely for his own endeavors. He scowled. Lord Burnley might have decided that it was the right time for him to wed, but Robert had no intention of doing so whatsoever. Given his good character, given his standing and his title, there would be very few young ladies who would suit him, and Robert knew that it would take a significant effort not only to first identify such a young lady but also to then make certain that she would suit him completely. It was not something that he wanted to put his energy into at present. For the moment, Robert had every intention of simply dancing and conversing and mayhap even calling upon the young ladies of the *ton*, but that would be for his own enjoyment rather than out of any real consideration.

Besides which, he told himself, *given that the* ton *will, no doubt, remember all that you did last Season, there will be many young ladies seeking out your company which would make it all the more difficult to choose only one, should you have any inclination to do so!*

"And are you to attend Lord Newport's ball tomorrow evening?"

Being pulled from his thoughts was an irritating interruption and Robert let the long sigh fall from his lips without hesitation, sending it in Lord Burnley's direction who, much to Robert's frustration, did not even react to it.

"I am," Robert replied, grimacing. "Although I do hope

that the other guests will not make too much of my arrival. I should not like to steal any attention away from Lord and Lady Newport."

Allowing himself a few moments of study, Robert looked back at Lord Burnley and waited to see if there was even a hint of awareness in his expression. Lord Burnley, however, merely shrugged one shoulder and turned his head away, making nothing at all of what Robert had told him. Gritting his teeth, Robert closed his eyes and tried to force out another long, calming breath. He did not need Lord Burnley to remember what he had done, nor to celebrate it. What was important was that the ladies of the *ton* recalled it, for then he would be more than certain to have their attention for the remainder of the Season – and that was precisely what Robert wanted. Their attention would elevate him in the eyes of the *ton*, would bring him into sharp relief against the other gentlemen who were enjoying the Season in London. He did not care what the gentlemen thought of him, he reminded himself, for their considerations were of no importance save for the fact that they might be able to invite him to various social occasions.

Robert's shoulders dropped and he opened his eyes. Coming to White's this evening had been a mistake. He ought to have made his way to some soiree or other, for he had many invitations already but, given that he had only arrived in London the day before, had thought it too early to make his entrance into society. That had been a mistake. The *ton* ought to know of his arrival just as soon as was possible, so that his name might begin to be whispered amongst them. He could not bear the idea that the pleasant notoriety he had experienced last Season might have faded already!

A small smile pulled at his lips as he considered this, his

heart settling into a steady rhythm, free from frustration and upset now. Surely, it was not that he was not remembered by society, but rather that he had chosen the wrong place to make his entrance. The gentlemen of London would not make his return to society of any importance, given that they would be jealous and envious of his desirability in the eyes of the ladies of the *ton*, and therefore, he ought not to have expected such a thing from them! A quiet chuckle escaped his lips as Robert shook his head, passing one hand over his eyes for a moment. It had been a simple mistake and that mistake had brought him irritation and confusion – but that would soon be rectified, once he made his way into full London society.

"You appear to be in better spirits now, Lord Crampton."

Robert's brow lifted as he looked back at Lord Burnley, who was studying him with mild interest.

"I have just come to a realization," he answered, not wanting to go into a detailed explanation but at the same time, wanting to answer Lord Burnley's question. "I had hoped that I might have been greeted a little more warmly but, given my history, I realize now that I ought not to have expected it from a group of gentlemen."

Lord Burnley frowned.

"Your history?"

Robert's jaw tightened, wondering if it was truly that Lord Burnley did not know of what he spoke, or if he was saying such a thing simply to be a little irritating.

"You do not know?" he asked, his own brows drawing low over his eyes as he studied Lord Burnley's open expression. The man shook his head, his head tipping gently to one side in a questioning manner. "I am surprised. It was the talk of London!"

"Then I am certain you will be keen to inform me of it," Lord Burnley replied, his tone neither dull nor excited, making Robert's brow furrow all the more. "Was it something of significance?"

Robert gritted his teeth, finding it hard to believe that Lord Burnley, clearly present at last year's Season, did not know of what he spoke. For a moment, he thought he would not inform the fellow about it, given that he did not appear to be truly interested in what they spoke of, but then his pride won out and he began to explain.

"Are you acquainted with Lady Charlotte Fortescue?" he asked, seeing Lord Burnley shake his head. "She is the daughter of the Duke of Strathaven. Last Season, when I had only just stepped into the title of the Earl of Crampton, I discovered her being pulled away through Lord Kingsley's gardens by a most uncouth gentleman and, of course, in coming to her rescue, I struck the fellow a blow that had him knocked unconscious." His chin lifted slightly as he recalled that moment, remembering how Lady Charlotte had practically collapsed into his arms in the moments after he had struck the despicable Viscount Forthside and knocked him to the ground. Her father, the Duke of Strathaven, had been in search of his daughter and had found them both only a few minutes later, quickly followed by the Duchess of Strathaven. In fact, a small group of gentlemen and ladies had appeared in the gardens and had applauded him for his rescue – and news of it had quickly spread through London society. The Duke of Strathaven had been effusive in his appreciation and thankfulness for Robert's actions and Robert had reveled in it, finding that his newfound status within the *ton* was something to be enjoyed. He had assumed that it would continue into this Season and had told himself that, once he was at a ball or soiree with the ladies of the *ton*, his exaltation would continue. "The Duke and Duchess were, of course, very grateful," he finished, as Lord Burnley nodded slowly, although there was no exclamation of surprise on his lips nor a gasp of astonishment. "The gentlemen of London are likely a little envious of me, of course, but that is to be expected."

Much to his astonishment, Lord Burnley broke out into laughter at this statement, his eyes crinkling and his hand lifting his still-full glass towards Robert.

"Indeed, I am certain they are," he replied, his words filled with a sarcasm that could not be missed. "Good evening, Lord Crampton. I shall go now and tell the other gentlemen here in White's precisely who you are and what you have done. No doubt they shall come to speak to you at once, given your great and esteemed situation."

Robert set his jaw, his eyes a little narrowed as he watched Lord Burnley step away, all too aware of the man's cynicism. *It does not matter,* he told himself, firmly. *Lord Burnley, too, will be a little jealous of your success, and your standing in the* ton. *What else should you expect other than sarcasm and rebuttal?*

Rising to his feet, Robert set his shoulders and, with his head held high, made his way from White's, trying to ignore the niggle of doubt that entered his mind. Tomorrow, he told himself, he would find things much more improved. He would go to whatever occasion he wished and would find himself, of course, just as he had been last Season – practically revered by all those around him.

He could hardly wait.

CHAPTER TWO

Stepping out of the carriage, her gown swishing gently around her ankles, Honora felt as though she were in an entirely different world to the one which she had known back at her father's estate. Being in London was overwhelming. Everything was so rushed, for there were always carriages trundling along the road, horses and their riders going past and people milling about along the street. Honora had been barely able to take her eyes from the view at the window for the first two days, as she and her aunt had rested from their journey to London. Her aunt, she had learned – for the lady had not stopped talking save to sleep and eat during their travel – had chosen to come to London to find herself a husband.

This had come as a great shock to Honora. Her aunt had been widowed these last few years, but Honora had never expected her to seek out another match. Lady Langdon had always appeared to be very contented with the situation her late husband had left her in, but now it appeared that she sought a little more for herself.

"Our first ball this evening, my dear Nora."

Honora turned her head and looked back at her aunt, who had only just stepped into the room.

"Good afternoon, aunt," she replied, turning to face her. "Is there something that you require?"

Lady Langdon laughed, shook her head, and dropped lightly into a chair.

"My dear, I have servants for anything that I should require," she said, pointing to a chair next to her, clearly expecting Honora to sit down in it. "Come, we have much to discuss."

Honora sat down quickly, looking at her aunt with slightly widened eyes, her hands clasping together tightly in her lap.

"As you may know, Honora, my late husband left me with a small house and a meager income," she began, to which Honora immediately frowned given that she knew all too well that the lady had a rather roomy townhouse in Bath - which Honora had visited only once but found to be more than satisfactory. "Therefore, I have decided to seek out a match for myself with a gentleman who can provide for me at the standard I require. The ball this evening *must* go well."

"I understand, aunt."

Honora searched her aunt's face for even a hint of compassion or consideration for Honora herself, but saw nothing but blankness in the lady's blue eyes. Her aunt was not at all in her dotage, although older than Honora herself by some margin, and given her beautiful, pale skin, thick, dark, glossy hair, and bright smile would attract the attention of some of the older gentlemen in London, Honora was sure.

Whilst I remain at the side of it all, watching and

longing and yet knowing that I will never be able to do as so many of the young ladies do.

"I do not know many here in London any longer, given that I am quite a bit older than those making their first entry into society – although their mothers may well be close in age to myself – but none will be seeking a match. I will require you, Honora, to be my companion so that I am never alone." She tossed her head, her curls bouncing, and gave Honora a warm smile. "It is a slightly unusual situation, I know, for most companions go to those who are well into their dotage, but since you could never find a suitable match, I thought this to be the best of things for us both."

A cold hand grasped Honora's heart.

"I could never find a match, aunt?" she asked, hearing her aunt's trilled laugh, and finding herself tensing at the sound. Anger and frustration swirled through her, but Lady Langdon appeared to have no awareness of this whatsoever.

"You *do* know that the *ton* is aware of your father's situation?" she asked, tilting her head and regarding Honora with a small, slightly condescending smile. "A gentleman would not even think of accepting you, my dear. But I am sure that you will enjoy London, nonetheless. And, of course, if it is required, I will be glad to keep you on as companion – or find you another position."

Honora knew that her aunt expected her to thank her for her condescension and kindness but found that she could not. Her lips were pressed too hard together and she could feel herself shaking gently. She dropped her gaze so that her aunt would not see the anger and the upset in her eyes.

"Well, this evening's ball shall be the very first we attend together!" her aunt declared. "You will remain by my side at all times, converse when you are spoken to - although

I shall make your position clear, so that no gentleman becomes confused!" Again came her trilled laugh and Honora squeezed her hands tightly together, forcing herself not to allow a sharp retort to fall from her lips. "I have purchased you three new gowns – they are respectable but nothing too fashionable. Make certain that you are presentable."

"I shall, aunt," Honora managed to say, now silently praying that her aunt would take her leave and allow Honora a few moments of quiet so that she might separate, consider, and work through each overwhelming emotion. "Of course."

Lady Langdon flashed a bright smile in Honora's direction, as though she had done her some great favor, before rising from her chair, saying one or two more things about the expectations she had for the evening, and finally leaving the room.

Just as Honora burst into tears.

"Now, here we are."

Honora took in a deep breath and, walking behind her aunt, made her way towards the grand townhouse. She had been greatly upset earlier that afternoon but had forced herself to find a few positive considerations in her new situation. Her aunt was not being deliberately cruel but rather, instead, appeared to think that she was doing Honora a great kindness in offering her this situation. Nor was she purposefully trying to upset Honora in stating the truth about her father's situation. She was doing so simply because it was the truth and she clearly thought that Honora needed to have an understanding of it.

Perhaps she is right, Honora thought as she climbed the stone steps. *I would not have a single gentleman so much as look at me, should I be here to make my come out.*

Taking a deep breath, Honora lifted her chin, tried to smile, and stepped inside.

The noise hit her like a wall, forcing her to catch her breath as she took a momentary pause just inside the house. She was not even in the ballroom yet and the sound of conversation, music, and laughter was already overwhelming.

"It is quite something, is it not?" Her aunt turned towards her, a broad smile on her face and a brightness in her eyes that told Honora she very much enjoyed the noise. "Do not worry, Nora. Everyone finds the ballroom to be somewhat intimidating when they first step inside!"

Honora managed a faint smile, appreciating this encouragement but still finding herself quite overcome with nerves. It took all of her inner strength to keep her composure as she finally approached their hosts and the receiving line, staying behind her aunt and praying that her curtsey would be quite perfect when the time came.

"*Do* excuse me."

Much to Honora's shock, a figure suddenly pushed past both herself and her aunt and then attempted to move forward at speed so that he could make his way to the receiving line first. It was astonishingly rude and even her aunt let out an exclamation which, at least, the gentleman in question turned in response to.

"Excuse me, *sir*," her aunt said, her voice high pitched and her frame suddenly very stiff indeed, "but what is the meaning of this?"

The gentleman turned to face Lady Langdon fully, his

hands spreading out to either side, as though he could not understand the question.

"I beg your pardon?"

"You have pushed me aside in some sort of attempt to garner entry to the ballroom a little more quickly, I presume," Lady Langdon stated, sounding a little angrier now, which, Honora thought, came solely from the gentleman's seeming inability to understand his wrong – although inwardly, she winced at the fact that her aunt had failed to mention that he had also physically moved Honora aside! Was he really so arrogant as to make his way past them without even being aware of the cost of his behavior? Did he think that his handsome appearance removed the need for good manners?

The gentleman clasped his hands together, then gave a short but stiff bow.

"I meant no harm," he said, his eyes fixed upon her aunt and giving Honora not even a single glance. "My sole intention was to make my way to Lord and Lady Yarmouth so that I might make my greeting."

Honora frowned, folding her arms and studying the gentleman steadily as dislike slowly began to creep up within her. Whoever this fellow was, she did not think that she believed a single word he had said thus far. He *had* to have been aware that his manner in pushing past them was both uncouth and disgraceful but had done so regardless. Why would he do such a thing? Did he truly think that he was more important than the rest of them? That Lord and Lady Yarmouth would be all the better pleased to greet *him* rather than Honora and her aunt?

Her eyes fixed themselves to the gentleman's rather smug expression. He had a long, elegant nose and slightly narrowed eyes – although whether they were held so because of the current situation, Honora did not know. His dark brown hair was combed neatly so that most of it fell to one side and his clothing was quite impeccable. Were it not for how he had behaved, Honora was sure that she would have thought him amiable as well as handsome, but now her consideration of him was already soured.

You are a companion, she reminded herself sternly, her hands suddenly falling to her sides. *You cannot speak openly to him even though you might wish it.*

That, Honora knew, was one of her failings. Her father had often brought it up during their years together, for Honora was inclined to speak her mind and to do so without hesitation. It had taken great inner strength not to send various retorts towards her aunt over the last few days and now, Honora called upon that strength again.

"And what is it that you think *we* are doing?" her aunt asked, as the gentleman's eyes suddenly caught Honora's, making her flush and turn her head away. "We too are seeking to make our way to Lord and Lady Yarmouth. Surely that was clear from the very beginning!"

The gentleman sighed heavily and dropped his head for a moment, sounding exasperated – and Honora could not help but speak.

"It is not at all gentlemanly to push oneself to the fore," she said sharply, not holding back her frustration and having no hesitation in dealing him a setdown. "And to jostle not only myself but my aunt in such a way is–"

"You clearly do not know who I am."

Honora's color rose as she narrowed her eyes, ignoring her aunt's attempts to break into the conversation. This gentleman was more than a little rude; he was disparaging, arrogant, and haughty and Honora's dislike of him only grew.

"I do not give a fig as to who you might be, sir," she said clearly, all too aware of her aunt's wide eyes. "If you are a high titled gentleman, then you may wish to act in such a way so that we do not think so little of your choice of behavior."

Silence spread between the three of them, but Honora did not drop her gaze. Holding her head high, she looked back at the gentleman steadily until, finally, he grimaced and returned his gaze to her aunt.

"Clearly, I did not either see you or give you my attention," he said, making Honora frown at his tone. The man was not regretful, nor did he attempt to give them even a single word of apology! It seemed as though he was determined to keep his pride in place at all costs. She dropped her head so that she would not have to look at the gentleman's arrogant face, linking her fingers together so that her hands clasped gently in front of her. The last thing that was required of her here was to say something more to him, despite just how much she might wish it. No doubt Lady Langdon was more than displeased with her already.

"No, you did not," her aunt snapped, harshly. "Now, permit us to make our way to our hosts so that we might greet them and pray do not attempt to hinder us any longer!" She threw one hand out towards Honora, who started at the sudden attention. "Come, Honora."

The gentleman turned to look at Honora more directly, but she remained in place, choosing to keep her eyes far from his in the hope that he would step aside and allow them both to pass. She heard a rattle of frustration emit from his lips but still did not look at him, turning now towards her aunt.

"But of course." The gentleman cleared his throat, opening one hand out towards their hosts. "On this occasion, I shall step aside and permit you to make your way to the receiving line whilst I take my place behind you."

The arrogance with which he spoke made Honora want to send a stinging riposte flying towards him but a quick glance at her aunt's sharp eyes still fixed to the gentleman, rendered her silent. Lady Langdon moved forward, and Honora went with her, marching past the gentleman, who had stood to one side, his head bowed, and one arm stretched outwards towards the receiving line.

"What a despicable gentleman," her aunt murmured, as Honora shook her head in disgust. "I cannot believe he thought to behave so!" Her eyes turned towards Honora. "Although you ought not to have said a word, Honora."

"That gentleman deserved his setdown, aunt," Honora replied, her voice lowering as they approached the receiving line. "I could not restrain myself."

She tensed, waiting for her aunt's reproach but, much to her surprise, her aunt smiled suddenly, chuckling for a moment.

"Indeed, he did," she replied, grinning and relieving Honora's fear all in one moment. "But not all gentlemen are as *he* is. In fact, he is the poorest of all poor gentlemen, and those, I am certain, are very few in number. How unfortunate that I should meet such a fellow at my first ball in London!"

"I am sure that you will soon meet someone much improved," Honora replied, coming to a stop just behind her aunt as their hosts began to greet the lady and gentleman before them. Taking in a deep breath, she set her shoulders and forced a smile to her lips. She had to forget all about that gentleman and, instead, focus on making a good impression on Lord and Lady Yarmouth. Even as a companion, she could not allow herself to behave at all improperly. It would reflect poorly on both herself *and* her aunt.

"Good evening, Lady Langdon."

Honora's stomach tightened as she waited for her aunt to introduce her. It took some minutes, for Lady Langdon seemed intent on conversing with Lady Yarmouth at length.

"Oh, and this is my niece, Miss Honora Gregory."

Lord and Lady Yarmouth looked towards Honora, who now felt so very nervous that it was difficult to even smile.

"Good evening, Miss Gregory," Lord Yarmouth said, smiling. "I recall your aunt informing us that you would soon be joining her in London."

"Good evening, Lord Yarmouth," Honora replied, dropping into her curtsy and all too aware of Lady Yarmouth's scrutiny as she tried to smile at the lady. "Lady Yarmouth."

Lady Yarmouth's eyes softened but it was to Lady Langdon that she spoke.

"My dear Lady Langdon, you have a beautiful niece," she said, her eyes still on Honora, although the compliment made her blush. "I am sure you will do very well, my dear. Is this your first ball? I am sure that Lord Crampton would be more than happy to dance with you."

Honora glanced behind her to where the gentleman who had been so very rude to her and her aunt now stood. The gentleman that Lady Langdon was now looking at.

"You are not introduced?" Lord Yarmouth asked, looking at Lady Langdon, who shook her head although her lips parted, clearly wanting to say something but having no opportunity to do so. "Ah, well then permit me to do so now!"

Honora's stomach twisted as she was forced to turn around and look directly into the eyes of the gentleman for whom she had nothing but disdain. The man looked back at her without even a flicker of interest in his eyes and nothing but tightness about his lips. It was clear to Honora that he had no eagerness to be introduced to her either.

"Might I introduce Viscountess Langdon, wife to the late Viscount Langdon, and her niece, Miss Honora Gregory."

Honora dropped into a curtsey, lowering her eyes as she did so.

"And this is the Earl of Crampton. Lord Crampton only came into the title a little before the beginning of last Season but has taken to the role very well indeed."

"How very good to meet you, Lord Crampton," Honora heard her aunt say, although a small smile slid across her face at her aunt's cool tone. She saw Lord Crampton's face color slightly, and he cleared his throat. His eyes darted from one side of the room to the other and Honora had to wonder if the gentleman was a little embarrassed.

"Good evening," he replied, bowing low, his tone grave. "I am very glad to make your acquaintance."

"And I am sure you would be glad to dance with Miss Gregory this evening?" Lady Yarmouth chipped in, sounding very cheerful indeed, as though she were doing Honora a great favor which, under any other circumstance, Honora would have been grateful for. She could do nothing other than lower her eyes, waiting for someone – anyone – to speak. There was no part of her that *wanted* to stand up with Lord Crampton but, given the circumstances, Honora knew that she could not refuse, nor show even a hint of disdain for the idea.

Lord Crampton cleared his throat again, giving himself a small shake, and then forcing a smile to his lips which did not bring even the smallest hint of happiness to his expression.

"But of course, Miss Gregory," he said, holding out one hand towards her. "I would be more than honored to dance with you this evening."

"That is very generous of you, Lord Crampton," her aunt broke in quickly, taking away the requirement for Honora to respond. "I do thank you for your consideration – as I am grateful for yours, Lady Yarmouth, but my niece is here as my companion and nothing more."

Moments of silence sent waves of mortification cascading over Honora. The shame of being so introduced was almost intolerable, and the urge to turn and run from them all began to chase her - but she knew she could not. Closing her eyes momentarily, she drew in a shaking breath and waited for what was to follow.

"Oh, pray forgive me," Lady Yarmouth said, clearly a little surprised, given the tone of her voice. "As your companion, did you say?"

"Yes, indeed," Lady Langdon replied, sounding much too cheerful. "I did not want to come to London alone and given that my brother has particularly difficult financial circumstances – circumstances which would prevent my niece from ever finding a match here, in the normal course of things – I thought to take her as my companion so that she would, at least, have a taste of London society." Honora glanced at her, seeing how her aunt pressed her hand to her heart, tipping her head as a small sigh escaped her. "I thought to be generous."

Lord Crampton cleared his throat gently but said nothing, making Honora's cheeks warm all the more.

"But of course, I quite understand." Lady Yarmouth smiled towards Lady Langdon, no longer looking at Honora. "Yes, how very generous of you to do so, Lady Langdon. I do hope that you *both* enjoy this evening."

The tightness in her throat prevented Honora from replying but, finally, her aunt took her leave and Honora followed quickly behind her, stepping away from their hosts *and* from Lord Crampton – for the time being, at least. Honora had not dared look at him ever since her aunt's explanation, finding herself much too ashamed to do so.

He has taken away your anxiety, at least, Honora thought to herself, as she followed her aunt through the open doors and into the ballroom. *Now you feel nothing but embarrassment.*

A small, wry smile spread across her face, and she stepped into her very first London ball – and caught her breath.

It was extraordinary.

There were so many people that Honora simply could not make them all out, seeing them as a blur of color and light. The music which was playing seemed to swirl between the laughter and hubbub of conversation, making her ears strain to make out one from the other. Everywhere she looked, there was a laughing face, bright eyes, or a broad smile – and Honora felt her lips curving in response. There was a wonderfulness here than she had not expected and it seemed to warm her very soul.

"Nora!"

She lifted her gaze and found her aunt frowning at her, beckoning one hand towards her. She tried to regain her composure so that she would not appear as a foolish young lady who could do nothing but stare and gawp at the scene around her.

"I must do what I can to reacquaint myself with a few of those I knew in past years," her aunt said, as she drew near. "You will remain with me and allow me to introduce you as and when I please."

"Yes, aunt."

Something heavy dropped into Honora's stomach as she realized that now, her aunt had yet another reason to keep Honora beside her – so that she might use her and her situation to improve her own standing in the eyes of others. So that they might think her generous, kind, and good natured in offering Honora such a position and, therefore, think all the better of her character. The ball might be wonderful, the music uplifting and the conversation delightful, but Honora felt nothing but disappointment and pain.

This was going to be a very difficult few months indeed.

CHAPTER THREE

*R*obert had not missed the growing dislike in Miss Gregory's eyes. Her green eyes had been hard and fixed for the first few moments, her lips flat and her brows low. Clearly, she thought little of him and that, in particular, made Robert very irritated indeed.

First, he had been forced to endure the complaints of Lady Langdon who had made such a fuss about Robert's attempt to make it to the receiving line before herself – which, admittedly, had perhaps been less than wise on his part - that Robert had been forced to step back and allow the two ladies to go before him. Had he not capitulated in such a fashion, then he would, no doubt, not have then done the very foolish thing, of asking a mere companion to dance with him. A companion who clearly did not know why he was to be so respected and who had allowed her frustration and irritation with him to show in her expression. He did not deserve that sort of disdain!

And I certainly was not pleased at being introduced in such a fashion. There is no need for anyone to know that I have only recently inherited the title.

He shifted his shoulders uncomfortably. There was always a little niggle, a small, irritating worry that he was being looked down upon by those in the *ton*. Having come into the title later in life, and from a situation where he had been neither poor nor significantly wealthy but had never expected to come into the title, Robert had sought to endear himself to society so that they would not notice any slight mistakes or unintentional blunders that he might make. The situation with Lady Charlotte last Season had been a most fortunate incident for Robert's sake, certainly, for to have the Duke and Duchess of Strathaven smiling upon him was lucky indeed.

I need not think of Miss Gregory any longer. Here, at least, I shall be recognized and spoken to by a good few people. With a broad smile on his lips which hid his shaky confidence, Robert made his way into the ballroom, making certain to turn to the right when he saw Miss Gregory and her aunt turn a little more to the left. He kept his expression genial, wanting to be seen as amiable and, of course, having every intention of appearing surprised and astonished when, no doubt, he was reminded of his actions last Season, by another.

"Good evening."

Robert inclined his head, bowing towards a young lady he recognized who, instantly, turned a little more to face him.

"Good evening, Lord Crampton!" she exclaimed, one hand snaking out to grasp hold of her mother's sleeve. "Mama, do you not recall Lord Crampton?"

The lady looked back steadily at Robert for some moments, pulled away from her conversation with another, older lady who, in return, was also studying Robert with sharp eyes.

"I do recall Lord Crampton, yes," came the swift reply as Robert bowed again, his smile spreading a little more as he waited for her to realize just *why* she remembered him so well. "Good evening."

"Good evening, Lady Arbuckle," Robert replied, remembering the lady at once. "You and your lovely daughter are returned for the Season, then?"

The lady nodded.

"We are," she replied, putting one hand to the small of her daughter's back, clearly encouraging her to face Robert a little more. The young lady obliged and turned away from her previous conversation partner entirely, leaving Robert feeling all the more pleased. "As are you, it seems?"

"Indeed, indeed," Robert replied, sighing, and waving one hand. "I could not stay away, although I confess that it is both difficult and wonderful to be in amongst the *ton* again – there are so many people that I wish to greet and, doubtless, so many who will wish to greet me also – that I do not think there will be enough time, even though there are still many, many weeks left of the Season!" He chuckled and Lady Arbuckle smiled in response, although that smile was a trifle uncertain, and Robert did not miss the way she sent a glance towards her daughter. A little confused, he then held out one hand to the young lady. "I do hope, Miss Swanson, that you might be willing to offer me the opportunity to dance with you this evening?" he asked, as the young lady then turned to look up at her mother questioningly. "I know I should be glad of your company."

His smile grew all the more as he saw Lady Arbuckle give her daughter a small nod, which she then took as agreement that Robert could dance with her. Within a few minutes, Miss Swanson had handed him her dance card and Robert accepted it quickly, thinking only to put his name down for one dance rather than two. After all, there were bound to be many young ladies whom he might wish to be in company with this evening and he could not spare any lady *two* dances! Two dances with any of them would only lead to speculation. Besides which, he considered, he would not take the waltz from any of them, for fear that whoever he danced with might think him a little more partial to her company – and Robert did not want that.

"The quadrille, Miss Swanson," he told her, handing back her card with a broad smile. "It has been some time since I danced, however. I must hope that my feet will remember all they must do!"

"I am sure that you will do very well indeed, Lord Crampton," Lady Arbuckle replied, as her daughter blushed and dropped her head so that her eyes were no longer fixed to Robert's. "Now, do tell me if the Duke of Strathaven has been in your company of late?" She eyed him carefully, tilting her head gently to one side. "After all, I am sure that the Duke and Duchess must still recall what you did to save their daughter!"

A warm glow of satisfaction began to fill every inch of Robert's being. He sighed inwardly with relief, his chin tilting just a notch as he spread out his hands to either side.

"Lady Charlotte has not yet returned to London," he said, speaking with a confident air which made it appear as though he were closely acquainted with the Duke and knew such things from private correspondence or conversation. "I am certain that they will be in London very soon, although it will take a little more courage for Lady Charlotte to make her way through society again, I am sure."

Lady Arbuckle's eyes widened.

"But of course, that is more than understandable," she said quietly, as her daughter listened carefully, her eyes flickering from Robert to her mother and back again. "That poor girl had such a dreadful ordeal."

"One that I was very glad indeed to be able to save her from," Robert replied, forcing a heavy sigh to his lips as he shook his head. "I am only disappointed and frustrated that it was required of me in the first place."

This was not the truth, however, but it garnered enough sympathy from both Lady Arbuckle and her daughter that Robert was secretly pleased. The truth was that, had he been anywhere other than in the gardens that night, then he would not have seen Lady Charlotte being pulled away against her will and would not have had need to act. He would still be a somewhat obscure gentleman, forced to make his mark on society in whatever way he could and struggle to find his place in a society that he knew very little of. That thought was a dark one and Robert pushed it aside easily enough. It had been a blessing for him that Lady Charlotte had needed his help, for it had pushed him into society's view and that had aided him in his attempts to settle into the *ton* without mocking whispers or biting words chasing after him.

"I am certain that she was very grateful to you, Lord Crampton," Miss Swanson murmured, her eyes holding fast to his, a slight pink in her cheeks. "I am sure that there are very few gentlemen with a character such as yours."

"You are very kind to say so, Miss Swanson," he replied, appreciating her compliment "I do want to assure you that such things do not happen very often and that you, yourself, will be quite safe this Season."

Miss Swanson nodded, although Robert noticed that she took a small step closer to her mother as she did so, perhaps a little more perturbed by what Robert had reminded her of than she wanted to express.

"I should take my leave," Robert continued, thinking that his time with Lady Arbuckle and her daughter ought to be brought to a close since he had many other young ladies to speak with and many other dance cards to sign. "Do excuse me. I will return for our dance, Miss Swanson, which I am already very much looking forward to."

She blushed, smiled prettily, and bade him good evening, allowing Robert to step away and, with a little more confidence now, begin to make his way around the ballroom, letting his breathing settle. The fear that he would be forgotten, that he would be pushed aside into the shadows and ignored by society was quickly fading away. Thanks to his connection to the Duke of Strathaven, Robert might continue to be sought after for the duration of this Season, and possibly even the next.

He shook his head to himself, recalling the first soiree he had attended. Entirely lacking in confidence, he had stayed near to the shadows in the room, had spoken very little, and had felt himself to be rather smaller than those around him – even those who had a lesser title than he. The urge to change that, to speak and act with confidence, had grown continuously, but it had not been until the evening with Lady Charlotte when he had been granted such an opportunity.

And had I not been there at the right time to save the lady, I might now find myself still that quiet, unassertive and reluctant gentleman whom no one cared to show any interest in. But now... He smiled, looking over his shoulder at Miss Swanson. Now, he had the *ton*'s attention, and he would fight to make sure he kept it.

For whatever reason, the incident with Lady Langdon and, indeed, with Miss Gregory, did not remove itself from Robert's mind despite his enjoyment of the evening. He simply could not forget it, nor the words she had poured on his head. Otherwise, the evening had, much to his relief, gone just as he had hoped. The many young ladies of the *ton* had been eager for his company and their mothers had, on the whole, brought to mind what he had done for the Duke's daughter last Season. For those who had forgotten, Robert was swiftly able to remind them of it by a simple word or two here and there, and then, within seconds, the accolades had come, and Robert's confidence had grown.

The dances he had stepped out for thus far had brought him nothing but delight, for the young ladies had been glad to be in his company and each had spoken of what Lady Charlotte had been forced to endure and what he had stepped forward to do without hesitation. They had all held expressions of gratitude and wonder as they had danced with him, their wide eyes held fast to his as though he were the very best of gentlemen.

Robert had enjoyed every single moment of each and every dance, his spirits lifted, his confidence full and his heart singing with the joy which came with their appreciation of him.

Only for his spirits to lower whenever Miss Gregory came to mind.

He watched her now as he sat quietly in a chair near the side of the room, able to have a mostly unhindered view. His thoughts were many, and he allowed each one to come in, one at a time. Of course, he reasoned, she was only a companion, and therefore would not know of what had taken place last Season. She would not have the same wonder and astonishment as the others he had spoken with, would not look up at him with wide eyes and gently curved lips. No, Robert knew that she had reacted to him very differently from the others and that, he considered, would have to be rectified. He had tried repeatedly to tell himself that she was a mere companion and that, as such, he ought to have no consideration for her opinion, but still, her attitude towards him and the harshness with which she had spoken railed against his heart and mind. It would *have* to be remedied.

Having now been studying her for a short while, Robert did consider the lady to be quite pretty, in her own way. She had not the timorousness which he might have expected from a companion, and he did not like the manner in which she continually let her gaze sweep from one side of the room to the other, making it plain that she was a little overwhelmed by it all. Her brown hair was glinting with hints of red and gold, her curls tumbling gently over one shoulder and that, at least, was pleasing. From what he recalled, her eyes were green and her lips a soft pink, although given that the former had been narrowed in his direction, Robert did not think that was particularly an asset to her. Perhaps it was that the education required to make her understand her place in the world and what her behavior ought to be thereafter had been somewhat lacking, for Robert was quite certain that no other companion would have spoken in the way she had done, regardless of the circumstances

Silently wishing that he could remove her from his mind entirely, Robert rose from his chair and began to make his way across the room towards her. It only took him a few steps and, from the way her brows lifted as he reached her, Robert assumed that she was a trifle surprised at his approach. He required only a few moments, he told himself – just enough to inform her of what he had done in saving Lady Charlotte, so that she would not again speak in such a way to him. It was very strange that her words should have diminished his confidence so, that they should reverberate in his mind in such a frustrating fashion, but Robert hoped that a hurried conversation now would bring an end to such troubles. A glance towards Lady Langdon told him that the lady was in deep conversation with a gentleman and his wife and did not seem to even notice his arrival.

"Good evening, Miss Gregory," he began, intending to launch into his explanation, but he was stopped short by the way that she tilted her head and narrowed her gaze.

"Are you quite finished studying me, Lord Crampton?" she asked, and a tightness came into Robert's throat as he stared back at her, not quite certain what to say in response. "It has been some minutes, has it not? Have you decided that you must now grant my aunt and I a decent apology?"

Robert could not immediately reply. His shock was much too great, his astonishment overwhelming him like a tight hand pulling him down backwards into a deep flood. He had not known that she had seen him watching, had not thought her even aware of his presence, and yet now, it seemed, she had been watching *him* in return!

He swallowed hard, a little surprised at the flush of heat which began to creep up his chest with the knowledge that Miss Gregory had been studying him. Blinking, he found himself looking down into her eyes and realized that they were green, as he had thought. *Green with a little hint of gold at the edges.*

"Ah, Lord Crampton."

Robert blinked quickly, bringing his attention to the older lady who now turned towards them, forcing a smile which he did not really feel and silently wondering why he had found himself so caught up with Miss Gregory in such a strange fashion

"Good evening, Lady...."

He winced inwardly, not able to recall the lady's title.

"Lady Langdon." The lady's brow furrowed as her lips flattened, pulling to one side. Evidently, Robert had upset her for what was now the second time. "Is there something you wished to say?" Robert cleared his throat, seeing both ladies looking at him steadily and finding his purposes suddenly thwarted. "You cannot have come to talk to my niece, surely?" the lady continued, as Miss Gregory's cheeks suddenly flushed red, and she looked away. "You are aware that she is my companion."

Robert nodded, his frame a little stiff.

"But of course, I do recall you saying so," he replied, finding himself a little flummoxed. For whatever reason, noticing the color of Miss Gregory's eyes had thrown all sensible thought from him and left him lost in confusion, as though he were groping around in the dark for a light. "Might I enquire as to who your father is, Miss Gregory?"

The question came to his lips unbidden and, despite having had no intention of asking it, Robert now turned back to the lady and looked at her questioningly, one brow lifting slightly as he struggled to hide his confusion from her. There was no particular reason for him to ask such a thing, unless it was that, for whatever reason, a part of him wished to know her true standing in society.

The lady did not smile, and in fact, there was a shadow in her eyes which made it apparent to him that her opinion of him was all the lower, given such a question. Robert tried to tell himself that such a thing did not matter and that, after this interaction, they need never speak to each other again, but still, her manner towards him had his toes curling in embarrassment at his own foolishness. Silently, he cursed himself for even coming over to speak to her in the first place. It had been unwise of him to allow her to capture his attention for so long, and ridiculous to allow it to fester in his mind. He ought to have simply set it aside and enjoyed the adulation of others, rather than think on the one young lady who had not responded to him in that manner. He did not need to converse with her ever again – so why was he here? Why had he found himself asking her such a question about her father? And why was it that he now found her eyes to be so very beautiful?

"My father is Viscount Greene, Lord Crampton," she said stiffly, her eyes glinting with steel as though daring him to make any remark on it whatsoever. "Although I cannot understand why such a thing would be of any importance to you."

His lips twisted and he opened his mouth to tell her his reasons, even though he could think of nothing to say.

"Viscount Greene is a good man and an excellent brother," Lady Langdon said, a little more sharply, as though she were afraid that he would make some disparaging remark about him. "If you have any further questions, *I* should be glad to answer them. My niece is here as my companion only."

"I did not mean any insult." He spoke hastily, finding that he was being quite honest. The desire to injure Miss Gregory was quite absent. It was as if she stirred an interest in him that he had only just discovered – an interest which he could not permit to grow any further. "Pray, forgive my question. It was not harshly meant."

Allowing his eyes to stray back to Miss Gregory, Robert held his breath, expecting her to be embarrassed at her aunt's bold remark, only to see a smile playing about her lips.

"Indeed, I think it would be best if my aunt continued your conversation, Lord Crampton," Miss Gregory murmured, tilting her head as her smile lingered. "Do forgive me, but I think I shall step back and permit you to continue your conversation in private."

Robert's dissatisfaction billowed like a flame caught by the wind. . It was clear from her smile, and the delight dancing in her eyes, that she had no wish to converse with him and was glad that her aunt would take over any further conversation. Her coldness towards him did not bring out either anger or the irritation that he had felt at the first, but rather a strange, unsettling frustration that begged him to resolve things between them. It was as if he did not want Miss Gregory to remove herself, as though he wanted her to continue to speak with him so that he might know her a little better.

Do not be so foolish. Your standing in society is excellent and you have managed to keep all whispers, gossip, and rumor about your previous situation in life far from you. Do you wish the ton to see your interest in a mere companion? They will say that your previous standing is coming to the fore, even though you are now an Earl! There will be whispers and mutterings about you. You must be careful.

Trying to smile, Robert cleared his throat and inclined his head.

"But of course, as you wish."

He waited for the desire for Miss Gregory's company to fade, but it only grew to the point that he could not ignore it - it was an itch which could not be scratched, could not be relieved.

He would *have* to do something about this strange

madness. Perhaps it would be best if he simply ignored Miss Gregory entirely. After all, her aunt was clear in her desire for him to speak only with her rather than with her niece, so therefore it would be wise to do as was requested.

There is no need for me to speak with her again. I will converse with Lady Langdon and thereafter, take my leave.

Opening his mouth, Robert made to say something more, only for the music to begin to swirl around them, reminding him of his next dance. Startled, Robert looked towards the orchestra, seeing them play the few notes and finding himself a little panicked that he would not find his next young lady in time.

"Miss Gregory. I fear you must excuse me now. I am promised for this dance."

"Good evening, Lord Crampton."

Miss Gregory's smile was, much to his surprise, rather warm and, as he looked into her eyes, he saw them sparkle. Something twisted in his heart, and he found himself mute, unable to form any sort of reply. It was clear that Miss Gregory was relieved that he was to leave her company and that was the very opposite of what he desired.

Closing his eyes, Robert pressed his lips together furiously, feeling his opportunity slip away. He could not stay here and insist on lingering in Miss Gregory's company, but nor did he want to depart when there was clear animosity and apathy in her heart towards him. He wanted the latter to change but did not know how to go about such a thing, nor why he felt such a strength of feeling after only a few minutes in her company. It was as if he had looked into her eyes and lost all of his sense in one, overwhelming, moment.

"Good evening, Lord Crampton," Lady Langdon put in, as Robert found himself bowing, the battle in his mind finally choosing one side. "I hope that you enjoy the rest of the evening."

With a harsh clearing of his throat, Robert turned on his heel and made his way through the ballroom, leaving Miss Gregory and Lady Langdon behind him. One hand was beginning to clench into a tight fist, whilst the other reached out to grasp a glass of wine and he paused only to throw it back, hoping that it might remove some of his confusion. The best thing for him to do would be to forget about Miss Gregory entirely. That which had just passed between them should be their final conversation. He had no need to speak to her again, had no need even to allow his thoughts to dwell on her – but his heart and mind refused to let her free.

CHAPTER FOUR

"I have received an invitation, Nora!"

Honora looked up from her book as her aunt sailed into the room, a letter waving in her hand.

"An invitation to take a walk in St James' Park with Lady Rutherford and her daughter, Lady Albina!"

"That is very nice, aunt," Honora replied, knowing that there would be no opportunity to read her book any further, given that she would now have to prepare to go for a walk. "It is good that the day is pleasant."

Lady Langdon's eyes were bright with excitement, as though *she* were the one who was in London for the very first time.

"We must make certain that I look my best," she said, coming across the room and tugging Honora's hand so that she rose from her chair, being led immediately from the room. "Lady Rutherford has a brother who is in London at present – the Earl of Sedgwick – and he may well join us!"

Honora's stomach twisted at this particular remark for it was a reminder that, once again, her time in London was here solely to focus on her aunt and her intention to marry again, should she be able to find another suitable gentleman for a husband. Honora sat down quietly on a chair as her aunt began to go through her various gowns and allowed her aunt's ongoing remarks about this afternoon's walk to drift over her.

She herself was sorrowful, Honora had to admit. There was also a growing awareness that she might soon find herself set up as a companion of another lady, should her aunt choose to marry, and that thought was not a pleasant one. If she allowed her mind to linger on it, Honora found herself so overcome with anxiety that she could not find even a flicker of hope or excitement. It was all much too overwhelming. To be in London ought to be exciting, even for a companion, but to know that she was to spend every moment making certain that she was doing things and speaking in the way that her aunt required was both exhausting and difficult. It did not help that her aunt was much too frank with those she met or was introduced to, for she always explained to them why Honora, despite being the daughter of a Viscount, was a companion rather than being a part of society herself. She had done it last evening in front of both their hosts and Lord Crampton, and each time it had driven pain directly into Honora's heart.

It is unlikely that you will ever have a Season, she reminded herself, her brow furrowing. *You must not forget that. Be grateful for this time in London.*

"I think that *this* would be the most suitable," Lady Langdon said, bringing over a walking dress which Honora agreed with immediately. "There is no certainty that Lord Sedgwick will be present, but it will be important I make a good impression upon Lady Rutherford regardless. She might tell her brother about me!"

"I am sure she shall," Honora murmured, giving in to her aunt's conceit. "And what do you require of me?"

Lady Langdon tipped her head and looked at Honora steadily for some moments, quietly assessing her. Honora remained silent, ready, and willing to do whatever her aunt asked of her.

"Lady Albina is Lady Rutherford's daughter," Lady Langdon said slowly, after a few moments. "Even though you are my companion, it would be beneficial for you to speak to Lady Albina and converse with her in a genial manner. That will allow myself and Lady Rutherford to speak openly."

A little surprised at her aunt's consideration, albeit for her own benefit, Honora nodded quickly, finding her spirits lifting just a little.

"Of course, aunt."

"You will be careful in what you say and what you reveal, Honora." A sharpness came into Lady Langdon's tone, her eyes a little narrowed. "There shall be none of the frankness that you shared with Lord Crampton last evening."

Flushing, Honora dropped her head.

"I understand, aunt."

"You have always had something of a sharp tongue and, whilst I am not at all in agreement with Lord Crampton's behavior last evening, you ought not to have said anything to him. I will not have that behavior demonstrated again."

Honora said nothing, her silence standing for agreement in her aunt's eyes. Lady Langdon did not appear to be at all upset that Honora had not been warm and friendly towards Lord Crampton but clearly disliked her response to him, thinking it unfitting for a companion.

"The man was very rude indeed, however, and I do not

think you need to make any effort to acquaint yourself with him further."

"I have no intention of doing so," Honora declared, raising her head and being entirely unaware that Lord Crampton had the opposite plan as regarded their acquaintance. "Lord Crampton, I think is also well aware of that feeling, aunt."

The hard glint left Lady Langdon's eyes.

"Good," she said, crisply. "Come now, let us make certain we are both ready for this afternoon."

Honora drew in a deep breath and rose from her chair.

"Of course, aunt," she said, making her way to her dressing table. "At once."

∽

"I AM VERY glad that you were able to accept our invitation."

Honora smiled at Lady Albina, thinking just how relieved she was that Lady Albina had been eager to converse with Honora and had done so with delight from the very first moment that they had stepped down from the carriage. She had asked Honora many questions and the conversation had flowed easily, allowing Honora to free herself of any lingering anxiety.

"It was to my aunt," Honora replied, "but I am grateful to be included. I am sure that you are aware of my present circumstances."

She shot a quick look over her shoulder towards her aunt who, of course, had made Honora's situation plain before they had even begun to walk with Lady Rutherford and her daughter.

Lady Albina laughed, shaking her head in a rueful manner.

"Your aunt does not seek to hold such news back," she said, looping her arm through Honora's as though they were very great friends already. Honora, surprised, looked across at Lady Albina, astonished that the lady should be so willing to be so readily acquainted with a companion. "I am sorry for it."

"Sorry?" Honora repeated, confused. "There is nothing that you have done to make this situation as it stands. My aunt is merely eager to make certain that no one mistakes me for an eligible match." Those words seemed to hurt her very soul as she spoke them, but Honora clung to her usual frankness, unwilling to be anything but truthful. "She is correct about my father's circumstances, although the situation is not of his making." Sighing, she looked away from Lady Albina, embarrassed to be speaking of her lack of fortune but wanting no ill to be placed on her father. "My late grandfather was not the most frugal of gentlemen and, unfortunately, these last few years have caused great difficulty with the fields. I know that if my father could bring me to London for a Season, he would."

"And that is what I am sorry for," came Lady Albina's eager reply. "It is not by your hand that you find yourself in this scenario. I cannot imagine what it must be like to be companion to your own aunt!"

Something about Lady Albina's remarks – mayhap her obvious kindness and sympathy – made Honora's heart soften, the truth of her situation bubbling up within her.

"It is trying," she replied, casting another glance behind her, for fear that her aunt would overhear her. "She is seeking a match of her own, if you can believe it." Seeing

Lady Albina's wide eyes, Honora laughed but nodded. "Tis true! I believe she wants a better situation than that which she has at present."

Lady Albina made an exclamation and turned her head, although Honora saw the anger that flared in her eyes. The only sound for some moments was their footsteps on the path, but Honora did not feel the need to break the quiet. Lady Albina clearly had some thoughts of her own.

"I find it most difficult to hear that your situation, such as it is, is not considered by your aunt, Miss Gregory," Lady Albina said, eventually, the spark still in her eyes. "I find that the *ton* as a whole is a most selfish creature and, unfortunately, that this only encourages that trait in each individual." She shrugged and Honora gave her a small smile. "It is a trait that I myself am determined not to have – and I shall certainly never wed a gentleman who has nothing but thoughts of himself."

This now explained to Honora the reason for Lady Albina's almost immediate friendliness and her complete absence of concern over Honora's status. Honora felt herself relaxing even more, silently thankful for this new acquaintance.

"And will you have to marry soon?"

Lady Albina sighed and rolled her eyes.

"This is my second Season and alas, I must now concentrate my efforts on making an excellent match." Laughing at Honora's confused look, she looked across at her with a warm smile on her face. "You think me a little ungrateful or foolish, mayhap."

"No, indeed not!" Honora exclaimed, not wanting to insult her new friend. "I am not –"

"I do not take any insult, have no fear," Lady Albina

laughed, pressing Honora's arm lightly. "It sounds a little odd, I am sure, to have a lady such as myself struggling to find even the smallest happiness at the thought of finding a husband. And yet, the thought of being alone, of being without a husband and having a dark and undistinguished future is also rather frightening."

Honora felt as though a burden had been lifted from her shoulders. Finally, she had someone she could speak with, someone she could share her own struggles with, and she was sure that, even with this early acquaintance, Lady Albina would understand.

"You cannot know just how relieved I am to hear you say such a thing, Lady Albina," she breathed, making Lady Albina look back at her with a growing air of curiosity. "I am greatly troubled by my own circumstances, although I have been attempting to find happiness and contentment in them. I had always hoped to have a Season but now I must consider what my future is most likely to be."

Lady Albina tilted her head, her eyes searching Honora's face.

"And there is nothing you can to do change your circumstances?"

Honora shook her head.

"Nothing that I can think of," she replied, a little heavily. "Besides which, my aunt has made it clear that she does not think any gentleman would be eager to court me, given that I have no dowry and a father who is impoverished – and might find himself destitute should the fields and the harvest fail again!" Her shoulders slumped, a heavy sigh falling from her lips. "I am a part of London society, yes, but I can never be a *true* part of it."

"I do not think that is true."

A little confused, Honora looked back at her.

"What do you mean?"

"Why not ask your aunt for the opportunity?" Lady Albina suggested, the idea throwing Honora off balance. "You say that she has all these reasons as to why no gentleman would think of you – but I am sure that there would be someone who would do so! You are beautiful and, I am sure, have an excellent character also. Mayhap a gentleman might find himself filled with affection for you!"

A laugh escaped Honora which she could not hold back, but Lady Albina did not join in. Instead, she frowned, her lips twisting a little. Honora dropped her laughter almost immediately, attempting to apologize.

"I cannot think that such a thing would ever take place," she began, but Lady Albina sliced the air with her hand, cutting her off.

"Why not ask for the chance to prove her wrong?" she said, as Honora tried to smile, thinking the idea preposterous. "That way you will be certain that you have done everything possible to change the future that awaits you otherwise." She smiled and patted Honora's hand as it rested on her arm. "And I could direct you towards gentlemen who want for nothing and could very easily be prevailed upon to fall in love."

This time, Honora's smile was genuine. It was almost too much for her to consider, for it felt as though it were a dream which was so far from what could ever be that Honora could not even let herself contemplate it.

"That would be very good of you, Lady Albina," she said, as her new friend smiled warmly. "I – I will consider the idea, certainly."

"Good."

Honora cleared her throat gently, wanting now to change the subject so that they no longer spoke of her circumstances. The idea that had been given to her was a little overwhelming, and Honora knew that she would need time to think through everything which Lady Albina had suggested.

"You must tell me which gentlemen you have met already, if there have been any."

At this, Honora laughed again, her mind immediately going to Lord Crampton.

"I have been introduced to one gentleman who I am not likely to forget!"

"Oh?" Lady Albina's eyes widened. "You have caught the eye of a gentleman already?"

Laughing, her green eyes dancing, Honora shook her head.

"No, I have not caught the eye of anyone, but have found myself entirely disinclined towards one particular fellow who behaved so rudely that both my aunt and I are completely averse to continuing in his company any longer!"

"Oh, and who might that be?"

Even the thought of his name had Honora's mouth setting tight.

"Lord Crampton."

Lady Albina's blue eyes widened, her alabaster skin suddenly flushing pink as she slowed her steps, staring at Honora in utter astonishment. Honora, who had no understanding of why her friend reacted this way, simply looked back at her steadily, but without speaking another word.

"Lord Crampton was the gentleman who behaved so very rudely to you and your aunt?" Lady Albina repeated, as Honora nodded. "You are quite certain?"

"I am," Honora replied, her eyebrows pulling tightly together as she frowned. "Why? Is there something wrong?"

Lady Albina finally resumed walking, shaking her head to herself as she did so.

"Lord Crampton is favored by the Duke of Strathaven," she told Honora, whose brows lifted so high in astonishment that they almost disappeared into her hairline. "He thinks Lord Crampton the very best of gentlemen and, indeed, Lord Crampton was hailed as the most wonderful, the most excellent of all gentlemen last Season."

"Good gracious!" Honora exclaimed, unable to put such news to what she herself knew of Lord Crampton and how he had behaved. "And why does the Duke think so highly of him?"

A small sigh escaped from Lady Albina's lips before she began to explain, as though she herself were a little jealous of what had taken place.

"Lady Charlotte, the Duke's daughter, was being stolen away by a nefarious gentleman who, I am sure, wanted only to marry her so that he might have her dowry and the wealth that, in time, the Duke would have given to her for her inheritance. This took place in the gardens of some gentleman or other – I forget his name – during a ball. Lord Crampton came upon this and rescued Lady Charlotte from the man who sought to compromise her and, thereafter, the Duke and Duchess of Strathaven have been in Lord Crampton's debt. I believe," she continued, as Honora listened in growing amazement, "that Lord Crampton laid such a blow upon Viscount Forthside that he knocked the fellow unconscious! Of course, thereafter everyone in the *ton* thought him to be the most marvelous fellow, and they all sought out his company. That attention might have waned a little over the last few months, but I am sure that society still considers Lord Crampton to be the most wonderful of gentlemen."

"I cannot quite believe it," Honora murmured, as Lady Albina nodded.

"He has not long been in London, I should say. I believe last Season was his first. By all accounts, Lord Crampton only took on the title of Earl a little over a year ago, after the death of the latter Earl of Crampton. It was a strange circumstance, from what I recall."

Honora tilted her head.

"Strange?"

"He was not at that time a titled gentleman nor had any expectation of inheriting a title. I believe the connection between him and the Earl of Crampton was something of an unexpected one, but it was proven to be quite proper. His father is the third son of the third son of the previous Earl's grandfather – and by some strange circumstance, all the male relatives before him were found to be deceased, so the title came to him."

"I see." This was rather interesting and despite herself, Honora found herself eager to know a little more. "So he has not been to Eton and the like?"

Lady Albina laughed.

"No, I do not believe so. His arrival had already sparked a good deal of interest and I believe there were some rumors about him, as the *ton* is always eager to do, but then the Duke of Strathaven declared him to be the very best fellow in all of London, and all such gossip faded away."

Blinking in surprise, Honora shook her head.

"Lord Crampton appeared, to me, to be the most odious, rude, and arrogant gentleman in practically all of London, and yet I hear something entirely different from you, and the Duke of Strathaven himself!"

"You will hear it from almost all of London, I am sure,"

came the reply. "I am glad I have been able to tell you about him before you said anything to anyone else!"

"I would not have done so, given that I am a companion and have no need for company other than hers, according to my aunt," Honora replied, a rueful smile on her lips.

Lady Albina laughed and Honora's lips curved gently, although her mind was whirring with this new and extraordinary news that Lord Crampton was not exactly as she had thought him.

Which then followed with another, more troubling question. Just how was she going to treat him now?

∼

"If that ODIOUS man attempts to converse with me this evening, I shall be very cross indeed." Honora could not help but smile at her aunt's determined exclamations. Lady Langdon tossed her head, her chin lifted just a little. "I do not care whether the Duke of Strathaven thinks highly of him or not, I have my own impression of him and thus, I am determined to continue to hold my own judgment."

"As am I, aunt."

Honora had, of course, told her aunt all that Lady Albina had said, and soon afterwards had seen the same surprise and astonishment on her aunt's face that she had felt. However, after a long monologue from Lady Langdon, it became clear that, to her mind, Lord Crampton was still to be considered both an arrogant and rude gentleman and, regardless of how he had behaved with the Duke of Strathaven, they were not about to fall at his feet and beg for him to allow them into a closer acquaintance.

"After all," her aunt had said, "just because a gentleman

has done one excellent thing does not mean that his character is at *all* favorable."

Honora had agreed wholeheartedly and had nodded her consent when her aunt instructed her to give only the smallest of responses to any conversation the gentleman might make, should he see them. The less time she spent in his company, the better – and what would be the most agreeable would, of course, be if she might never speak to the fellow again! After all, Lady Langdon had made it quite clear that *she* was the only one who was worth Lord Crampton speaking to and, whilst the sentiment injured Honora a little, she was relieved that he would, most likely, not approach her.

"If he were a little older, I would not even allow myself to consider him as a potential match!" Lady Langdon declared, a bright smile on her face as she looked around the ballroom, portraying a happiness that she clearly did not truly feel. "Quite why he wished to speak to you, I cannot imagine!"

"No, nor can I, aunt," Honora replied, a little dully. Her aunt was, once more, speaking all that was in her heart and mind without even the smallest consideration for how Honora herself might feel. She bit her lip and looked away. Despite her lack of good opinion of Lord Crampton, there had been a slight flush of awareness that had come over her when she had seen the way he watched her. It had been a somewhat astonishing moment, for no gentleman had ever looked at her in such a way and the knowledge of it had thrown her heart into a furious rhythm whilst warmth had curled in her belly. She had dismissed it at once, of course, but the awareness of it still lingered. "I am sure that he will not approach us."

Her aunt threw her a vague smile before turning her attention back to the ballroom.

"Now, Honora, Lord Leatham is to be present this evening."

"Yes, aunt?" Honora replied, aware of whom Lord Leatham was since her aunt had been introduced to him at the previous ball – and Honora had been introduced also, although only with a passing glance.

"You are to watch for him and, should you see him, inform me at once," her aunt ordered, as Honora merely nodded in silence. "*Particularly* if he is alone and not in conversation."

"I shall, aunt."

"Good evening, Miss Gregory, Lady Langdon."

Turning her head, the bright and ready smile that Honora had placed on her lips instantly fell away as her eyes came to rest upon none other than the very gentleman she had been hoping to avoid. Her heart sank as she looked into his eyes, seeing him attempt to smile whilst still, somehow, managing to frown.

Why did he approach if he did not wish to speak to me? Honora thought to herself, commanding herself silently to smile and then, thereafter, to drop into a quick curtsey.

"Good evening, Lord Crampton," she murmured, as her aunt too quickly greeted him, sending a slightly sharp glance towards Honora which encouraged her to say very little by way of conversation.

"This looks to be a pleasant evening, does it not?" Lady Langdon said loudly, drawing the man's attention. "A delightful one, in fact."

"Yes, I think it will be a very pleasant evening," Lord Crampton murmured, his eyes darting about the room as though he were surveying the group of gentlemen and ladies present and wondering just how many of them would be agreeable to him.

Honora caught herself frowning as Lord Crampton suddenly caught his lip between his teeth, giving the appearance of a gentleman who was a little less than confident. The expression was gone after only a moment, but Honora clung onto it, finding herself a little surprised. Perhaps there was more to Lord Crampton than it appeared – although quite why she would have any interest in that, she could not understand.

You are a companion and here only to assist your aunt. It would be best to keep any and all thought of Lord Crampton far from your mind.

"Aunt, I can see Lady Rutherford and her daughter," she said softly, her eyes flaring so that her aunt would catch her meaning. "Did you not say that you would meet her this evening?"

Lady Langdon's smile was a moment or two in coming but, when it did, it was with an obvious and sparkling relief that flooded her expression.

"Alas you must forgive me, Lord Crampton," she said, as Honora felt the full warmth of her aunt's relief in being able to step away from Lord Crampton. "I can see my friend, and I did promise to go to her the very moment we arrived. Pardon me."

Honora lowered her head and made to follow her aunt, glad that they would not have to linger in Lord Crampton's company, only for the gentleman to reach out and catch her arm.

"Miss Gregory."

She was unable to move past him, her arm still in his tight grip as she lifted her head, looking first towards her retreating aunt and then to Lord Crampton thereafter. Her aunt had no awareness of Honora's concern, and she was left staring up into Lord Crampton's eyes.

"I–"

He looked at her confused, his lips pulling to one side as he looked down at where his hand rested on her arm as though he had not expected to behave so.

"Miss Gregory, I apologize."

His hand dropped from her arm and Honora, instead of swinging on her heel and hurrying after her aunt, merely looked up into his face. There was a frown adorning Lord Crampton's brow and, as he pulled his hands behind his back, he cleared his throat and shuffled his feet, giving the impression of a gentleman ill at ease.

"But of course."

She made to turn but Lord Crampton spoke again.

"I behaved poorly at our first meeting, Miss Gregory. I apologize. I shall, of course, make certain to apologize to your aunt also." Honora blinked in surprise, her stomach turning over on itself. After all, she had said and discussed with her aunt as regarded Lord Crampton and their decision that he was *not* to be considered, talked to, or even acknowledged unless they had no choice to do so, she now found herself quite at a loss as to how to address him. This was most unexpected. "I shall not keep you from your aunt." His frown lifted and a small smile pulled at one side of his mouth although his eyes remained grave. "Excuse me."

She watched him take his leave, her heart beating in wild confusion. It took her a moment to turn on her heel and go after her aunt and, even as she did so, Honora could not stop herself from looking over her shoulder after him, managing to do so at the very same moment as he looked behind him towards her.

Their eyes met and a streak of warmth ran the length of Honora's frame, making her blush furiously. Turning her head sharply, she caught up with her aunt and, keeping her head low, stood quietly to one side, with her hands clasped loosely in front of her. But her mind whirled furiously, and her heart continued to pound at the most ridiculous pace. Whatever was she to make of him now?

CHAPTER FIVE

"I do not think I have ever seen you so troubled over a lady."

Robert sighed and wondered if he ought to have brought this matter into discussion in the first place. After a sleepless night, he had risen early and, even though he had attempted to sit at his study desk and work through his correspondence, had done nothing other than stare blankly at an untouched piece of paper. When Lord Venables had come to call, Robert had ended up talking to him about Miss Gregory – although Lord Venables was entirely unaware of the lady's situation.

"You behaved poorly, and you apologized. Is there any need for this mental torment?"

"No, there is not. That is why I am so very frustrated with myself."

Lord Venables swirled his glass of brandy but kept his eyes fixed on Robert.

"What is it that you wish of her? It is not as if you have any intention to marry."

Snorting at the idea, Robert shrugged.

"She ought to mean nothing to me, I know." Raking one hand through his dark brown hair, he forced himself to tell Lord Venables the truth. "She is a companion!"

Lord Venables' mouth fell open and he stared at Robert in silence for what felt like many minutes. Robert, aware of the heat rising up his neck, turned his gaze away and wondered if he ought not to have said anything at all.

"A companion?" Lord Venables spluttered, his eyes wide as Robert threw back the rest of his brandy, feeling the fire of it burn down his chest. "You are this frustrated over a *companion*?"

"She is a lady!" Robert protested, as though that made any particular difference. "She is the companion to her aunt, who is here, I believe, to make another match if she can." Seeing Lord Venables' lifted eyebrow, he sighed and shook his head. "Miss Gregory is the daughter of a Viscount who has very little financial security at present and thus, she is now the appointed companion of her aunt. A little strange, I grant you, but that is as it stands."

"Which still does not answer my question as to what it is about her that has you so caught up with her?"

Robert groaned, tilting his head back against the chair and closing his eyes.

"I found myself eager for her to know what had occurred last Season. I found her manner towards me at our first meeting to be intolerable."

Lord Venables sighed and shook his head.

"That is an explanation, certainly, but not one that I particularly like," he mumbled, as Robert sighed and quickly signaled the footman for another brandy.

"It is not the full explanation, however." Closing his eyes, Robert spread out his hands to either side of himself. "I believed her to be in the wrong. I thought that if I approached and told her of my standing in society such as it is now, then she would not think to treat me so again. But the moment I drew near, I found myself... a little confused."

Lord Venables' brows lifted.

"Confused?"

"And I have been so ever since, to the point that I apologized to her last evening! I do not think that I had any intention to do so but that was what came out of my mouth."

A broad grin settled over Lord Venables' face.

"Mayhap that was what was in your heart, but you deliberately chose to ignore it. I am all too aware of just how much your standing in society means to you, and her manner must have been displeasing." He shrugged. "But it was foolish for you to allow it to affect you so, given that she is a companion. You acted foolishly, and whilst you might not have wished to have apologized, I believe that doing so has done you a great benefit. To retract that apology would be utterly ridiculous and I must hope you are not intending to do so, given this confusion you speak of?"

Robert grimaced.

"No, of course I am not."

"Good." Lord Venables slapped his knee. "Then you must simply remove her from your thoughts and this confusion will fade into nothing. It is about strength of mind and that is something you lack at present, I think."

Lord Venables had been one of Robert's first acquaintances in London and he had proven himself to be a decent fellow. Whilst Robert was glad of Lord Venables' company, he was also all too aware of the fellow's penchant for speaking without even the smallest hindrance. Lord Venables took great pride in speaking against what others seemed to think, sometimes choosing to play the part of their adversary whilst, at other times, doing so only to make them think a little more or simply for his own pleasure. Robert did think him a good friend, but oftentimes wished that his friend was not as frank as he knew him to be. This, of course, was one of those moments. Lord Venables knew of Robert's struggle with society. He knew of Robert's difficulty with his confidence and whilst he understood that Robert sought acceptance from the *ton* by way of buoying that confidence, he had never encouraged Robert in seeking society's approval.

"I fear I shall have to take my leave," Lord Venables said, before Robert could say another word in his own defense or in an attempt to explain himself further. "It is late, and I am to host a dinner party tomorrow."

Robert was surprised.

"Tomorrow?" he asked, as Lord Venables nodded. "But you are only just in London! You have organized such a thing already?"

His friend chuckled, rising to his feet and, before he answered, throwing back the rest of his brandy in one gulp.

"I thought it best to make certain that my closest friends and acquaintances knew of my return to London," he said, as a tight hand closed into a fist around Robert's heart. "Besides, you know that I am very much inclined towards company." He chuckled, then placed one hand on Robert's shoulder. "You will find your invitation arriving tomorrow morning, Crampton. Do not look so upset."

Having not thought that his expression was at all perturbed, Robert quickly rearranged his features and then laughed, albeit somewhat tightly.

"I thank you," he said, as Lord Venables continued to grin. "I shall take my leave also, I think."

"And tell me, what shall you do, regarding the lady?"

Lord Venables asked as they both walked towards the door of White's.

Grimacing, Robert shrugged, but chose not to respond, narrowing his eyes as he attempted to find his carriage in the darkness. Lord Venables' coachman called out, coming towards them both with a lantern in his hand.

"Ah, there you are, my good man," Lord Venables said, pleasantly. "Capital. Now, we should just make certain that Lord Crampton has found his way and then we can take our leave."

Robert chuckled ruefully.

"I fear that my coachman is not at all as practical as your own," he replied, thinking silently to himself that he ought to encourage his coachman to do much the same, the next time he was to return to his carriage in darkness. "That is kind of you, I thank you."

The coachman nodded, turned, and began to lead them back towards where the waiting carriages stood, giving Robert enough light to see by and to identify his own carriage quickly. His coachman, it seemed, was fast asleep, given the way that his head lolled forward, and his shoulders slumped. Robert rolled his eyes, sighing heavily in frustration.

"Shall I light your lantern, my Lord?"

Robert, grateful for the assistance, gestured for the man to do so and, after a moment, Robert himself was holding a lantern and lifting it up towards his coachman.

"I shall depart," Lord Venables said, one hand on Robert's shoulder for just a moment. "Do look out for that dinner invitation."

"I shall," Robert agreed, turning back to his friend, seeing his features shrouded in shadow. "Thank you."

Lord Venables grinned.

"I do hope you can rouse your coachman," he chuckled. "Good evening."

"Good evening," Robert muttered, turning his attention back to his coachman and growing irritated that he was still not awakening. There was a footman also but, for whatever reason, he did not appear to be present. Growing all the more frustrated, Robert held up his lantern high and began to call out to his coachman, who still did not move.

"I shall dock your wages," he muttered aloud, thinking that even that ought to rouse the fellow but, again the man simply did not move. It was more than frustrating, and Robert began to consider whether or not he ought to find himself another coachman altogether, sighing as he set the lantern down on the ground with the intention of climbing up towards his coachman to waken him.

His footing was unsure, and Robert slipped more than once, cursing under his breath as he did so. This was not what a gentleman ought to need to do. This was not the behavior of a gentleman either and yet, here he was, attempting to climb up to his coachman to force him into wakefulness. Gritting his teeth, Robert finally reached his driver and grabbed at him hard, his anger overflowing.

"Whatever is the matter with you?" he asked, shaking the man with a good deal of force. "Wake up at once!"

The coachman did not respond, and a bolt of fear slammed through Robert's heart. Why was the man not moving? Why were his eyes refusing to open? Swallowing hard, he looked around him but could see nothing, for the dim light of the lantern he had left on the ground barely permitted him to make out even a single feature of the man before him.

And then something caught hold of him, hard. It was not the coachman, Robert was sure of it, and before he could let out any sort of exclamation, any sort of shout of anger, the hand which now held him released him and, instead of pulling him forward, pushed him back.

Robert felt himself falling, and his hands reached out to grasp onto something – anything – so that he might be able to prevent himself from crashing to the ground, but he grasped naught but air. In a moment, Robert found himself slammed back hard onto the cobbles, pain shattering through his head and his back. A long, agonized groan came from his lips but there was no one nearby to hear it.

His eyes closed as Robert fought back against the pain and the black wave of unconsciousness, struggling to hold himself away from it. His ears were ringing, his whole body burning with the impact upon the cobbles. He could do nothing, see nothing nor hear anything aside from the sound in his ears, but Robert was slowly becoming aware that there was someone else present. His mouth tried to form words, his strength going entirely into calling out for whoever it was, only for the unconsciousness to take hold of him completely. His eyes, which had been fluttering in an attempt to open, finally closed completely, his body going limp and his strength fading away.

He was lost.

~

"My Lord?"

Robert opened his eyes, the pain growing steadily in his head as he tried to focus on who – or what – was in front of him.

"It *is* he," he heard someone else say, his eyes closing tightly again at the light which seemed to be trying to bore a hole into his skull. "I did tell you –"

"Yes, Nora," Robert heard the second voice say, sounding a trifle irritated. "Oh, would that our coachman had not stopped! We might already be home and retired to bed!"

Trying to say something, Robert could only let out a long groan which, he could tell, pushed both of the ladies back from him at once. He tried to lift his hand but found his arm so stiff and sore that he could only raise it a fraction.

"We should try to help him into his carriage," he heard the first voice say, his mind feebly attempting to recognize it. "Or I could make my way to White's? There are sure to be –"

"You cannot go in there, Nora!" the other lady exclaimed, her voice seeming to be much too loud for Robert's pained head, for he winced and let out yet another groan.

"Then send the coachman!" the first lady told the second. "We cannot do such a thing on our own, aunt. It is just as well that our coachman stopped, else I do not think anyone would have seen him until morning!"

An exclamation of frustration came from the second lady's lips.

"And it would have been his own doing, I am sure," he heard her say, as the urge to profess himself quite innocent of such a charge rose within him. "To drink so much as that is quite excessive! His coachman...."

Her voice faded away, giving Robert the impression that the lady had turned away and was now talking from a distance – a distance which was much too far for Robert's still ringing ears to hear clearly.

He did not know what happened next. There was a commotion and all manner of noises, from running feet to loud exclamations and grunts of understanding. He felt strong hands lift him, trying to set him on his feet, but there came such a yelp of pain from his lips that he was quickly laid out on a soft material which Robert soon realized was the seat of his own carriage.

"Something more is the matter, I am sure," Robert heard the first voice say. "Lord Crampton appeared to be in a good deal of pain."

"Which is to be expected," he heard the second say, "given that he has, no doubt, fallen backward into unconsciousness in his drunken state. Now, where is his coachman?"

The door was closed then, and Robert heard nothing more, his head still pounding and his mouth unable to form any clear words. He wanted nothing other than to be able to sit up and demand to know exactly what had taken place, to tell them all that he was not foxed and had not caused himself to fall backward, but the only thing he found the strength to do was to open his eyes a little more.

The carriage was warmer than the cold ground he had been lying on and, as it began to roll away, Robert wondered just who was driving it. What had happened to his coachman? Where was his footman? And just who had pushed him back so that he had fallen with such a great force onto the cobbles? Agony began to twist into his back and Robert shifted carefully, his lips pressed tightly together so that he would not let out any sort of exclamation. It felt as though every single bone in his body was burning with pain, as though every sinew was pulled far beyond its capacity. He wanted to twist and turn in the hope of removing the pain, but even the smallest movement was difficult.

I will have to find these ladies and give them my explanation, he thought to himself, his battered pride pushing itself to the forefront of his mind. *If only I knew who they were!*

No doubt he would be able to find out the names from his coachman – if that is who was driving his carriage. Else, he had only the name of 'Nora' to go on, and that was not much help. Robert's brow furrowed all the more, afraid that the rumors of his supposed intoxication would spread around London with great speed, leaving him to attempt to dampen them with a poor, lackluster, and almost unbelievable explanation for what had taken place.

What had *actually happened?*

Robert's eyes fluttered closed, his mind whirring whilst still trying to battle through the pain which ricocheted through his body. He had no knowledge of what had happened, no real understanding of what had taken place. All he knew was that someone, somehow, had set a trap and he had walked straight into it. He just did not know why.

∽

THE FOLLOWING MORNING, Robert was feeling a little better. His body was still sore, and his head still ached furiously, but there was, at least, enough strength in him to rise from his bed, dress, and make his way to the dining room to break his fast.

"Where is my coachman?" he asked, the very moment that the butler came into the room, a silver tray in his hand. "I must speak to him at once."

The butler nodded, setting down the tray in front of Robert without a word before leaving the room just as silently as he had come in. Robert glanced at the letters with a disinterested eye, having no inclination towards reading any of them. Picking one up, he set it aside before turning the second over, seeing Lord Venables' seal. The corner of his mouth lifted. His friend had not forgotten his promise to send Robert an invitation to his upcoming dinner party, and Robert had every intention of accepting.

"Mr. Hobart, my lord."

The coachman, Robert noticed, was looking incredibly pale. The man's eyes were bloodshot, his hands twisting his hat over and over in front of him as he kept his head low in deference. Robert's eyes narrowed. Was the man feeling guilty about his actions last evening?

"What happened?" he asked, sharply. "I tried to waken you and…." Trailing off, he shrugged one shoulder, spreading his hands wide. "Well?"

Mr. Hobart shook his head.

"I don't know, my Lord," he said, his words so quiet that Robert struggled to hear him. "I was waiting for you to arrive, and a footman came out of White's, offering me and your footman a drink."

Robert's frown deepened.

"A drink?" he repeated, unbelievably. "You mean to tell me that you *and* the footman were offered a drink by a footman from White's?" Seeing the coachman nod, he let out a snorted exclamation. "And where did such drinks come from? Who paid for them?"

"I don't know, my Lord, but neither me nor Jenkins – that's the footman – thought to ask. We just accepted them, as it was late and…." The man closed his eyes tightly. "The next thing I know, someone is slapping me awake and I hear that you have had some sort of accident."

The butler cleared his throat gently, choosing to interrupt Robert's conversation with his coachman – much to Robert's astonishment.

"If I might, my Lord, I should give some credit to what

Mr. Hobart has explained," he said crisply, making Robert's brows lift – not only in astonishment at being so interrupted, but also with the boldness with which his butler spoke. "Jenkins, the footman, has become very ill overnight. The doctor has come to see him and declares that he has taken something which has caused his stomach to roil and twist in a most painful fashion."

"But *you* do not have such difficulties?" Robert asked pointedly, only for the coachman to shake his head.

"I have risen from my bed to be summoned here, my Lord," he replied, just as Robert noticed a sheen of sweat across the man's forehead. "Jenkins was still unconscious for a long-time last night, my Lord. He has only just woken up."

Robert ran one hand over his forehead, a little confused.

"If that is the case, then where was he?" he asked, as the footman and the butler exchanged looks. "I did not see him last evening when I came to waken you."

Mr. Hobart pressed his lips together tightly, whitening them.

"He was in the carriage, my Lord," he mumbled, clearly aware that to have a servant wait in the carriage itself was not something that he ought to have permitted. "It was not a particularly warm night and Jenkins is nothing more than skin and bone!"

This did not upset nor frustrate Robert, who merely shrugged one shoulder in response, given that he had a good deal more to think on.

"I see. So, he was still in the carriage when we returned home?"

Nodding, Mr. Hobart dropped his head even further, so that his chin practically rested on his chest.

"On the floor of the carriage, my Lord."

"I see." Given that he had been disinclined to believe

Mr. Hobart from the beginning, Robert now began to recognize that it would be foolishness to force himself to believe that there was nothing more than drunkenness on the coachman's part. It seemed that someone had been eager to make certain that Robert could not easily find his way home and that, in climbing into the driver's seat as he had done, he had then been easily injured. Sighing, he lifted his chin and spread his hands. "It seems that you and Jenkins are absolved of any responsibility for last evening," he said, firmly, all too aware of the relief which etched itself across the coachman's features. "I am certain that there was someone eager to injure me, and that both yourself and Jenkins stood in their way. Therefore, the drinks were sent out to you by such a person and, no doubt, contained something which would render you both unconscious. When I came to the carriage, they knew that I would be forced to attempt to waken you and, in climbing up towards you, could then be pushed from it." The coachman's wide eyes caught his for a moment, horror held fast within them. "I do not know who such a person might be, nor do I need you to even attempt to guess," Robert continued, waving a hand in dismissal. "I shall ask you, however – and you may pass this onto Jenkins also when he recovers – to be much more vigilant in the future."

The coachman nodded, clearly relieved that he was not about to be dismissed from his position.

"But of course, my Lord. I am just glad that Lady Langdon and her companion were present to help."

A cold sweat broke out across Robert's forehead as he looked hard at the coachman, realizing now that the man knew precisely who it was who had come to Robert's aid. He had not even thought to ask him and now, it seemed, he had to face the difficult truth that it had been none other than a young lady who already thought very little of him.

Robert fought the urge to throw back his head and groan, choosing instead to clear his throat rather abruptly, causing the coachman's hands to tighten on his hat.

"Yes," he murmured, "they were of great help. You are dismissed."

He waved a hand in the man's direction, with the butler already making his way to the door and the coachman soon following after. He waited until both men had left the room before he dropped his head into his hands, his elbows resting on the table.

Why had it been Lady Langdon and Miss Gregory? They already thought poorly of him - and the fact that now, no doubt, Miss Gregory would think all the worse of him was somewhat upsetting. Despite his apology to Miss Gregory, he had not managed to say a word to Lady Langdon and could not be certain that Miss Gregory herself had even accepted his words. Besides which, he had no idea himself, of who it could have been to put such a plan to injure him into place, nor of why they might have been so eager to do so. It simply did not make sense and yet, Robert had to admit, there was a twinge of fear in his heart now. He did not want to be continually afraid of going out into society, worried about what might happen to him should he, for example, accept a drink from the hand of another.

That would be a return to how I was when I first came to society – uncertain and unsure. Closing his eyes tightly, he shook his head. *I cannot be that way again, but this has stabbed hard at the confidence that was growing within my heart.* His head throbbed a little more strongly and Robert winced, pushing his hands through his hair before resting his head back.

"This was a purposeful act, and I shall discover who has done such a thing and why they behaved so, to make certain that they cannot injure me any further."

The confidence in his voice was not in his heart, however, for Robert knew that such a task was almost insurmountable. He could not even think what he might have done to upset someone to such a grave degree as to cause them to act so. Was it someone jealous of his success in his acquaintance with the Duke of Strathaven? How could he whittle it down to only one gentleman? And how was he to stay safe in the process?

CHAPTER SIX

"I, for one, do not know what to think."

Honora nodded slowly, considering.

"Nor do I, aunt," she murmured, still astonished at what had occurred the previous evening. "He appeared quite foxed!"

Her aunt tutted and shook her head.

"It is ridiculous for a fellow to behave in such a fashion, even if it is late in the evening," she stated unequivocally. "What would he have done if we had not been present? Why was his coachman seemingly so incapacitated?"

That, Honora had to admit, was the question which was, at present, continuing to bother her. The coachman of Lord Crampton's carriage had been, it seemed, fast asleep and thus had not attempted to help his master – but Honora had watched as one of the footmen from White's had been forced to employ a great deal of effort in rousing the fellow. And Lord Crampton, whilst clearly injured and hurting from his fall or collapse, had been struggling to speak even a word of sense, which meant that neither man had been able to give any explanation of what had taken place. She had simply been forced to watch the carriage move away, with Lord Crampton inside, and his still swaying coachman up on the box, with only the dim light of the lantern to guide their way. Regardless of her somewhat convoluted feelings as regarded Lord Crampton, Honora did hope that he had been able to return home safely.

"I am fatigued because of his reckless nonsense, for it quite put me out of sorts last evening," Lady Langdon sighed, placing one hand, palm outwards, to her forehead in a somewhat pathetic gesture, which made Honora smile inwardly. Her aunt would soon shake off her supposed weariness so that it would not prevent her from fulfilling the rest of her day. Any plans which had been made by the lady would continue regardless.

"And are you too fatigued to go into town as you had planned?" Honora asked innocently, tipping her head in a gesture of inquiry.

"Oh, but of course not!" Lady Langdon exclaimed, dropping her hand. "After I have enjoyed a few afternoon calls – for I am certain there shall be some – we shall make our way to Hyde Park for the fashionable hour." She smiled satisfactorily at her niece. "Things are going very well, I think, and I am sure that Lady Albina will be there so you might have the opportunity to converse with someone."

Honora smiled. For whatever reason, last evening's adventure with Lord Crampton seemed to have brought about a slightly increased intimacy between herself and her aunt. This was the first time that her aunt had mentioned something which Honora might consider without speaking about how it would impact herself personally.

You could ask your aunt for the opportunity.

The suggestion that Lady Albina had placed in Honora's mind suddenly roared to the surface and Honora's smile faded, her stomach twisting.

"You are not eager to speak to Lady Albina?" her aunt queried, one eyebrow lifting in a slightly irritated gesture, as though Honora ought to be more than grateful for the chance to speak to someone other than her aunt.

"Oh no, aunt, I am looking forward to seeing her again," Honora replied quickly, fearful that Lady Langdon might take the opportunity away again if she thought Honora ungrateful.

The following silence was broken by a tap at the door, and her aunt's frown immediately deepened, given that it was not yet time for afternoon calls. However, with a small glance at Honora, she turned back and then called for the servant to enter.

"My Lady, there is a note for Miss Gregory."

Honora froze in place as her aunt stared back at the servant, saying nothing. The seconds ticked by as Honora's whole body tensed, having no knowledge of who might have written to her, and certainly understanding her aunt's astonishment.

"Are you quite certain it is for Miss Gregory?" Lady Langdon asked, her voice cracking with tension, only for the servant to nod, shooting a quick glance towards Honora before dropping her head.

"It is perhaps from Father."

Honora spoke, trying to smile at her aunt who, eventually, nodded and gestured to Honora, before turning her back and making her way to the window, looking out at the scene below. Her back was straight, her shoulders tense and Honora knew that she would be waiting to see just who had written to a mere companion.

Taking a deep breath, Honora accepted the letter, broke the wax seal, and began to read.

What she read quite astonished her – to the point that her gasp of surprise caught Lady Langdon's attention and shattered her intention to leave her niece to read her letter alone and uninterrupted.

"What is it, Nora?" she demanded, as Honora stared down at the letter in utter astonishment. "Is there some sort of bad news? Is your father unwell?"

"No, aunt, it is not from my father," Honora murmured, her eyes fixed on the final few lines before she turned to look up at her aunt, praying that she would not be angry. "It is from Lord Crampton."

Her aunt's expression changed in an instant.

"Lord Crampton?" she repeated, her eyes narrowing and her brows pulling together. "Whatever is that odious man saying? And why is he writing to you?"

Honora looked down at the letter, unable to answer the latter question.

"He is asking if we might call on him and states that, whilst he would be glad to have called upon us here instead, he cannot do so at present, given the pain which lingers in his frame."

"Pshaw!" Lady Langdon exclaimed, waving a hand as if there were a bad odor which had come into the room. "He has no one to blame for that but himself! What does he wish to hear from us – from you?" She eyed Honora sharply. "Has he written to you in the hope of garnering sympathy, knowing that I am less than inclined to grant him such a courtesy?"

"I cannot tell, aunt," Honora replied calmly, for whilst she was more than astonished at the letter, she had to admit to feeling a twinge of curiosity within her heart. "He states that it is to explain last evening and finishes by writing that he is, of course, in our debt and would be more than appreciative if we could attend him as he asks."

"Arrogant fool!" Lady Langdon cried, spinning on her heel, and marching across the room as though she wanted to take herself as far away from the letter as she could. "To think that we – that *I* – would be willing to do that!"

Honora hesitated, looking up at her aunt for a moment before deciding to be honest.

"I should like to hear what he has to say, aunt." She winced under her aunt's sharp gaze, which was suddenly thrust towards her, knowing that she was angering her, but choosing to continue in her usual honest manner. "You are quite right in your suggestion that he has written to me in the hope of gaining my sympathy and, therefore, our acceptance, I believe," she said, hoping that this would placate her aunt a little, "but the truth is, I should like to know what happened. It was a very unusual situation and –"

"You have no right to make any demands of me, Honora." Honora pressed her lips together, dropping her head and feeling shame begin to creep into her heart as her lowered status was, once more, brought to the fore. She had no doubt now that Lady Langdon would refuse absolutely and was annoyed with herself for encouraging her aunt's ire. A long and frustrated sigh poured from Lady Langdon's lips. "I find Lord Crampton's arrogance and pride truly dislikeable, but I do not want him to do harm to my reputation. He does, no doubt, want to make certain that we will not spread rumors of him and if I do not attend as he has asked, there is the chance that he might choose to repay my discourteousness by speaking ill of me. Therefore," she finished, as Honora lifted her head, "we will go."

Honora's astonishment knew no bounds.

"Thank you, aunt."

"But I will not sacrifice my own afternoon calls *or* my visit to Hyde Park!" Lady Langdon stated, finally sinking into a chair. "It must be tomorrow. Or the day after that."

"Tomorrow," Honora agreed, rising so that she might pen a response to Lord Crampton immediately and a little surprised at the relief and gladness that entered her heart. "Thank you, aunt. I am sure that Lord Crampton will be grateful also."

Lady Langdon merely rolled her eyes at this, and Honora hid a smile, making her way from the room and wondering silently just what it was that Lord Crampton would have to say, and also thinking that it a little surprising that she was looking forward to seeing him again.

∽

"Good afternoon."

There was a stiffness in Lord Crampton's movements which could not be hidden and yet, still, he managed to lift his chin a little higher as both Honora and her aunt entered his parlor - as if he did not want either of them to notice

"Good afternoon, Lord Crampton," Lady Langdon said crisply said, as Honora murmured the same. "Thank you for receiving us."

Honora expected him to thank them for calling, to thank them for replying to his note, but Lord Crampton said neither, gesturing for them both to sit down where they pleased. Exchanging a glance with her aunt and seeing the tightness about Lady Langdon's jaw, Honora sat down carefully and then looked expectantly at Lord Crampton, her fingers twisting together as she held her hands in her lap. In the shadows of the room, his dark brown hair appeared almost black as it fell across his forehead, there were dark smudges under his blue eyes and a tension in his jaw and across his lips which left her in no doubt as to how he was feeling.

"Let me ring for tea." Lord Crampton tugged the bell pull and then, finally, sat down himself, his fingers coupling together as he looked from Lady Langdon to Honora and back again. Honora waited expectantly, finding herself interested in what the man had to say by way of explanation and finding herself somewhat concerned for him. He had never appeared this contemplative, nor so silent, before and Honora's concern only grew with every moment. She remained quiet, however, having been instructed by her aunt to say very little and allow Lady Langdon to work her way through the conversation. After all, her aunt had reminded her, she was a companion and a companion only. It was not her place to go speaking with any gentleman she chose, even *if* that gentleman had invited them to his home.

"You were going to speak to us about last evening, I believe?"

Lady Langdon's voice was high pitched, her expression frozen in a look of disdain. Lord Crampton nodded and opened his mouth, only for the door to then open to permit the maid entry, bringing through the tea tray. It was clear by the exasperated sigh which fell from Lady Langdon's lips that she was frustrated by the delay, but Honora used the opportunity to study Lord Crampton a little more. Whilst she was here, in *his* abode, she found herself becoming more interested in who Lord Crampton was. He was, as far as she was concerned, rather ordinary, with nothing to make him appear radically different from any other gentleman of London. Just because he was in good favor with a Duke did not give him any greater importance in her eyes, although he was the *only* gentleman who had made his way into her thoughts – wanted or otherwise.

"Might you pour the tea, Miss Gregory?"

Honora blinked in surprise as Lord Crampton asked her such a thing, looking sharply at him but seeing his head turn directly towards her aunt in what she took to be a dismissive gesture. Smarting from what, to her mind, was a clear lack of consideration and the horrid awareness that this was to be expected of a companion, Honora lifted her chin and sent him a hard look.

"I am afraid I am unable to do so at present," she said clearly, drawing Lord Crampton's attention in an instant. She watched his frown darken his features but felt her own lip curling, angry with him for his dismissive attitude "I do beg your pardon."

Lord Crampton opened his mouth but then closed it again with a snap. His eyes caught hers but quickly looked away as he cleared his throat in a gruff manner. Honora said nothing further and gave no explanation for her inability to do such a thing, returning his look with a mere lift of her eyebrow. Lady Langdon, much to Honora's surprise, did not appear to be at all angry with Honora's decision to behave so, for upon her lips there came a small, triumphant smile. Honora's spirits lifted and she shook off her dissatisfaction and simply waited for him to act.

Eventually, Lord Crampton did sit forward and begin to pour the tea without a word – although Honora noticed the stiffness in his arms and the way that he pressed his lips together tightly as he did so. In an instant, guilt washed over her, and her shoulders dropped. Regret seared her heart, making her face flush with embarrassment. *What if he asked me to do so simply because he is in pain and would find it difficult to do so himself?* Her eyes closed tightly as shame burned her cheeks. She had not even considered such a thing but had been fully resolved that he had asked her to pour the tea simply because of her lowly status. In her frustration and upset, she had simply reacted and now was ashamed of her response. Was it that she did not wish him to think of her a companion? And if that was true, then why should she *want* him to view her as only a young lady of the *ton* and not the companion she truly was?

"I wanted to thank you – and to explain – about last evening," Lord Crampton began, his tone flat as he handed Lady Langdon her cup of tea, keeping his gaze towards her rather than looking back at Honora. "I believe that it was you who came to my assistance."

"Yes, it was," Lady Langdon stated, her words clipped. "It was very fortunate for you that my coachman chose to drive by White's – and that he stopped as he did."

There was no mention of Honora, no word about what she had done and how she had been the one to insist upon caring for Lord Crampton, and Honora felt herself sink down into her chair a little more, as though she were naught but a shadow.

Lord Crampton nodded but did not smile.

"I should not like to leave you with the impression that I was foxed," he said, getting directly to the point as he finally handed Honora her cup of tea with only a mere flick of his eyes in her direction. "That was not the case."

Lady Langdon threw a quick, unimpressed glance towards Honora but Honora nodded, choosing to believe his words to be true, despite her aunt's obvious disbelief.

"I see," Lady Langdon replied, a wryness in her tone which could not be hidden from Lord Crampton himself. "Then I do hope that you are recovered from whatever malady it was that overtook you."

Lord Crampton's brows drew together, and Honora caught the flash of anger in his eyes. It was clear to him that her aunt did not believe him and that was causing him great upset. Honora tilted her head, looking back at Lord Crampton steadily, and waited until he finally caught her gaze before she spoke, pushing her own embarrassment away and praying that he would be willing to speak to her despite her previous sharpness.

"Might I ask what took place, Lord Crampton?" she asked, seeing him nod as the shards in his eyes began to melt away. Was there a look of appreciation, of gratitude, in his face now? "Did you injure yourself?"

"I was pushed."

Honora's eyes flared wide in bewilderment as she looked back at him, seeing the steadiness in his gaze and the way his jaw worked for a few moments.

"You were pushed?" Lady Langdon repeated, sounding entirely unbelieving, but Lord Crampton did not so much as look at her but rather held Honora's gaze instead. It was as if he were grateful to her for her questions, for her trust that he spoke the truth.

"My coachman was, it seemed, asleep. When he would not waken, I was forced to climb up to the box in an attempt to rouse him. When I managed to reach him, an unseen foe pushed me backward. That was the reason for my seeming lack of conversation – not through drunkenness but rather through naught more than a great deal of pain and a struggle against unconsciousness." Honora blinked rapidly, trying to sort through the surprise and shock which rippled through her. She knew that her aunt would not give even the smallest credence to Lord Crampton's explanation, but that could not be said of her. There was something about such an explanation – as ridiculous as it sounded – that, to her mind, held the truth. Lord Crampton's gaze returned to her aunt. "I do not know who the perpetrator was but wanted to express my gratitude to you for your help, as well as to make certain that you did not think too ill of me."

"I have no intention of telling any other about what we witnessed last evening, Lord Crampton," Lady Langdon said clearly, setting down her teacup and raising her chin just a fraction so that she looked a little more down her nose towards him. "That is not the sort of lady I am, nor the sort of young lady my niece has been raised to be. Whatever took place last evening, we are both very glad that you are not terribly injured, and we do hope that your recovery comes to its end very quickly indeed." Honora noted that her aunt had begun that particular statement by referring only to herself but had then gone on to include Honora. A small sense of relief and gladness lifted her heart and, again, Lady Albina's suggestion came to her mind. "And now we must take our leave."

This was the end of their conversation and their time with Lord Crampton but, as her aunt rose, Honora was surprised at the surge of eagerness to either remain in his company or continue speaking with him. After her own foolishness in refusing to pour the tea, she now considered that there was more to Lord Crampton's character than she had first believed. Her first impression of him had been of an arrogant, selfish gentleman who cared naught for anyone but himself – and whilst there was some truth in that, for certainly he *was* arrogant and eager to impress, Honora was beginning to discover an eagerness to know him a little better.

"We should not want to weary you, since you are still to recover fully," her aunt finished, as Honora reluctantly rose to her feet, disappointed that they were to take their leave. "Good afternoon."

Honora bobbed a curtsey, lowering her gaze and choosing not to give him so much as another glance, for fear that he might see the disappointment in her eyes, before turning on her heel and following after her aunt. The door was opened for them by a footman who was, it seemed, clearly able to hear all that was going on within the drawing-room and had been able to open the door promptly, and Honora was just about to make her way through it, when she heard Lord Crampton speak.

"You are upset with me, I think."

Honora stopped short, seeing her aunt sailing out of the room but finding that she could not take another step without speaking openly to Lord Crampton.

That trait of speaking bluntly and honestly in her interactions came again to the fore and she turned back towards him, a dull heat burning in her cheeks.

"Indeed, Lord Crampton, you are quite perceptive" she replied, seeing the way his eyes flickered. "I was a little upset over your request to pour the tea, but I realize now that I was mistaken to feel so affronted."

"I did not mean to upset you." His voice was low, and he dropped his head, his hands clasped tightly behind his back. "It was not because I thought to dismiss you." Her stomach tightened and she pressed her lips tightly together, the silence becoming heavy between them. "I must hope that you also will not speak to any other about what you witnessed."

Her eyes shot to his, a tension beginning to radiate through her frame.

"I beg your pardon?"

Has he stopped me only to make certain that his standing in society will not be tainted?

"It is discretion I seek."

Her eyes closed and a jolt of anger pinned her in place, her jaw tightening.

"Miss Gregory?"

Honora shook her head, frustrated that he had seemingly no awareness of his behavior and how his words had affected her.

"I pray that reason was not your main purpose in calling us here, Lord Crampton?"

"I do not know what you mean."

"Yes, you do," Honora shot back, her hands tightening into fists as she fought to control her sudden burst of anger. "You have asked us here to thank us, of course, but you also fear that your standing in society could be damaged, should either my aunt or I speak of what we saw, is that not so?"

He shrugged one shoulder.

"I wanted to make certain that the truth was known to you both, although of course, that was not my main reason for requesting your company."

"And what, might I ask, was your main purpose in doing so?"

Lord Crampton looked back at her steadily and, much to Honora's astonishment, his hand reached out momentarily as though he wanted to take hers. Then he closed his eyes, gave a small, rueful smile, and shook his head.

"I wanted to thank you," he said simply. "I apologize if I have offended you. I shall not keep you any longer, Miss Gregory. Good afternoon."

CHAPTER SEVEN

"I believe I greatly frustrated the lady." Lord Venables lifted one eyebrow as Robert expressed his displeasure over Lady Langdon and Miss Gregory's recent visit and his own foolishness in treating Miss Gregory in such an off-hand manner. "I confess that I should like to pretend that I do not understand why I behaved in such a way, but it is clear to me that my pride had a great deal to do with it. I did not want her to know that my injuries pained me so and thus, I spoke in that ridiculous manner – and received her sharp retort in response!'"

"I think that it takes a great deal of bravery to say such things to a gentleman of your standing, particularly given her situation," Lord Venables replied mildly, as Robert winced. Lord Venables let out a chuckle, lines around his eyes forming gently. "You do not like me saying such a thing either, I have no doubt, but that is the truth of it."

"Your opinion is of value to me, Venables. What frustrates me the most is that I *did* want to thank both herself and Lady Langdon for her help as well as make certain that they knew the truth so that they would not think ill of me."

"And would not spread *their* truth around London," Lord Venables finished which, despite himself, Robert knew he could not argue with. The last few sentences Miss Gregory had spoken had burned a guilt into his heart which, as yet, he had not been able to forget. She was a companion and yet, he had chosen to write to her rather than her aunt – and then he had treated her with a little dismissiveness and thereafter, had made it appear as though his interest in his own self-preservation as regarded the *ton* was of more importance than ensuring that they were thanked. He had unintentionally brought pain and shame to her heart by doing so – and therefore, had proven himself unworthy of her kindness.

That he could not seem to forget. It tore at his heart and made him suddenly all too aware of his pride.

"Ah, good afternoon, Miss Johnston, Lady Farquhar."

Pulled out of his thoughts, Robert was quickly in conversation with both Lady Farquhar and Miss Johnston, the latter of whom was looking at him with slightly widened eyes. Robert felt his prolonged thinking as regarded Miss Gregory begin to fade as Miss Johnston's gaze became fixed on his, her cheeks coloring gently.

"And, of course, we have heard that the Duke of Strathaven has returned to London."

Robert turned his eyes towards Lady Farquhar, his heart quickening and his interest suddenly sparked.

"The Duke of Strathaven has returned to London?" he repeated, as Lady Farquhar nodded. "When?"

"Why only two or three days ago," came the reply. "I would have thought that you might have been aware of it, given that you are so closely acquainted with the Duke!"

A small fire of embarrassment ignited in Robert's soul, but he forced it away as he pasted a smile to his face

"Ah, but alas, I am very far behind with my correspondence," he said, struggling to find an excuse. "I am recently recovering from an injury and, as such, have been unable to give my correspondence the importance it deserves."

"I quite understand," Lady Farquhar replied, tilting her head. "Although I am sorry to hear that you have been injured."

"As am I," Miss Johnston murmured, catching Robert's attention again. "I do hope that it was not serious?"

He smiled at her, pleased when her cheeks colored all the more.

"It was not at all serious, no," he replied, making her smile. "I thank you for your concern."

"I am sure that you must have injured your hand terribly when you struck down that gentleman – the one who was stealing Lady Charlotte away," Miss Johnston continued, her voice dropping low as though she were afraid to mention it for fear of bringing unpleasant memories to Robert's mind. "But it was a very great rescue, I have heard. I know that Lady Charlotte must be forever in your debt."

For whatever reason, this did not bring with it the usual delight to Robert's spirit. Instead, a vision of Miss Gregory suddenly floated in front of his eyes, pulling his thoughts back towards her. Perhaps it was the lingering guilt that came, over how he had handled her visit with her aunt yesterday, or the slowly growing realization that his pride was, in fact, of greater importance to him than he had ever really understood.

"I am sure that every other gentleman in London would have done as I did," he said waving a hand in an attempt to dismiss the matter. "I thank you for your concern over my present injuries, however. I am soon to be quite recovered."

Miss Johnston let out a small sigh, her hands clasping together as she looked up at him with admiration shining in her eyes. Robert swallowed, throwing a glance to Lord Venables and seeing his friend frowning at him. Perhaps he too had expected a very different response from Robert.

"And what has become of Viscount Forthside?" Lady Farquhar asked, as Lord Venables shrugged one shoulder and turned his attention back to the lady. "Does anyone know whether or not the Duke thought to call him out after his attempt to steal Lady Charlotte away?"

"I know he did not," Robert replied, having been a little surprised at the Duke's reluctance to do so. "Viscount Forthside simply retreated to his estate, from what I am aware. I do not think that he will return to society."

Lady Farquhar nodded gravely.

"It would be best if he did not," she agreed, firmly. "But you, Lord Crampton, I am sure, will be glad to see Lady Charlotte again?"

Her eyebrow lifted, her question hanging in the air, and it was at that moment that Robert realized what she meant.

He cleared his throat.

"I confess that I am not particularly well acquainted with Lady Charlotte," he replied, seeing how the lady looked back at him in surprise. "I was glad to be of assistance, certainly, but there is nothing but the smallest of acquaintances between us." He smiled warmly. "But she is an exceptional young lady, from what I have heard."

Catching the glance shared between mother and daughter, Robert put his hands behind his back and dropped his head. This was all very strange. Only a few days ago, he would have been profoundly grateful and indeed, very interested in Miss Johnston's company, for he would have reveled in her admiration of him. Now, however, that did not seem to have as much importance as he had once given it. It was as though his continued acquaintance and practically constant consideration of Miss Gregory had revealed a part of himself that Robert was not certain he liked. A part of him that now made him consider conversations differently.

Soon, however, farewells were made, and Robert continued on his way with Lord Venables, trying to push away his strange melancholy.

"You do not intend to court anyone this Season, do you?"

Robert shook his head. "I do not think so, no." *Why does Miss Gregory's face come to mind at such a time?* He cleared his throat as if doing so would push her away. "Why do you ask?"

Lord Venables' lips pulled to one side.

"You did not respond to Miss Johnston in the way that either I expected or have previously seen.".

Robert looked away, a tightness pinning his chest.

"Indeed."

He did not make any further remark but Lord Venables, it seemed, was not yet finished speaking.

"After the incident with Lady Charlotte, I have seen you eager to garner as much attention from the *ton* as possible. That was simply to bolster your pride, was it not?" he asked, as Robert blinked in surprise, having not expected to hear such words from his friend. "You delighted in all that was offered you. Rather than seek out one particular lady, you hoped for many of them to come in search of you, to flatter you and to make you feel as though you were just like any other gentleman of London, if not better."

"That may well be so."

His friend cast him a sidelong glance, but Robert did not look at him.

"You know that I will be honest with you. I have found the eagerness in your heart to continually seek out the flattery of others to be both tiresome and difficult. However, given that I believed I understood your reasons for doing so, I have never chosen to say a single word."

Robert coughed gruffly, his tight chest making it difficult to pull in air.

"You understood?"

The shame of such a thing began to sear across his skin but Lord Venables did not remain silent, perhaps heedless to all that Robert now felt.

"You were brought into the title without ever having had any expectation of ever being the Earl of Crampton. You were not given the same education as most gentlemen and were fearful that the *ton* would speak cruelly of you. Consequently, your fear drove you and when the incident with Lady Charlotte occurred, you found yourself thrust into a very happy situation, where the Duke of Strathaven thinks highly of you. The *ton*, therefore, must also think the same."

Finding that his tongue was a little big for his mouth, Robert licked his lips, aware that his heart was beating a little more quickly.

"This is a most awkward conversation, Venables," he said, gruffly. "Perhaps we need not go into such particulars."

"Why? Because you do not like it?"

Robert closed his eyes and turned to face his friend, ending their walk.

"That is precisely why. I have enough torment considering Miss Gregory and now you too are adding to my burden!"

"I do not mean to do so." Lord Venables set his hand on Robert's shoulder, making him flinch. "Miss Gregory does not treat you with the same admiration that you have been offered from every other young lady of the *ton*. You have found yourself caught up with her because of that behavior, is that not so? And in doing so, she has forced you to consider your character and your situation in ways you have not done before." Dropping his head, Robert fought the urge to run one hand over his eyes. He did not like speaking with such honesty, particularly when his thoughts were already in such disarray. "If it is true that you have no intention of marrying, then I should make you aware of the injury you may cause some of the young ladies of the *ton*."

Robert lifted his head.

"Injury?"

Lord Venables nodded, his eyes grave.

"These young ladies will be hopeful that you might choose one of them for your bride. It might be best if you made it plain that you have no intention of marrying this Season."

"I – I have never thought about such a thing before."

Lord Venables dropped his hand and sighed.

"Indeed. As I have said, I do not wish to injure you, nor make your difficulty all the greater, but given that you find yourself struggling with Miss Gregory's remarks and, mayhap, your feelings for the lady in question, it seems a wise opportunity to speak openly with you. The young ladies that compliment you so very often and look at you with such admiration are the ones who are hopeful for your particular interest. This may be another moment when you realize that you have thought only of what their remarks do for *your* state of mind without giving any consideration to what they might seek from you instead."

Robert ran one hand over his eyes, choosing to sit down on a wooden bench next to some petunias. The beauty and the perfume of the flowers brought him no joy, however, for he was much too caught up with what he had heard from Lord Venables. The truth was throwing some heavy weight down upon him and Robert struggled to shoulder the burden.

"I have always been very afraid that the *ton* would reject me." Mumbling, he spoke half to himself, half to Lord Venables. "It seems now that this fear has continued, even though the Duke's particular friendship gave me more standing in society than I had ever hoped for."

Lord Venables sighed and shook his head.

"I have set too much on you, I think."

"No, I am grateful. I have much to think on." Looking up, Robert gave his friend a small smile. "I think I shall sit here for a time."

"Are you quite certain? We could make our way to Whites and—"

"No, please, I beg you. I am quite contented here."

He smiled and assured his friend for the third time before Lord Venables took his leave.

Robert sighed and closed his eyes tightly. Just how did society view him? Did they think of him as an arrogant, overly confident fellow who sought out the attention of others but gave them nothing in return? His unwilling heart began to accept that he had a prideful appearance, one that covered his ongoing fear that he was not as the rest of the gentlemen in society and that, one day, someone would recall his past circumstances and the unusual ascension to the title and would spread rumors and gossip about him.

That would make him shrink inwardly, to cling to the shadows as shame and embarrassment poured onto his head and thus, to ensure that such a thing never took place, he had tried to find a way to make certain that society always thought well of him.

But I have injured others in doing so.

"Lord Crampton."

He looked up sharply, his eyes widening as he saw none other than Miss Gregory before him, her cheeks dappled by the shadows of the leaves above them which danced in the afternoon sun. Her aunt was nowhere to be seen and, much to Robert's astonishment, she appeared to be quite alone. She was gently strolling along the path and clearly had only the intention of greeting him before continuing on her route, but Robert was there beside her in an instant.

"You need not accompany me, Lord Crampton." Her tone was a little tight, her eyes darting to his for only a moment before slipping away. "My aunt is only a few steps away. I believe that she is conversing with an acquaintance for a few moments. It is a conversation that she did not wish me to overhear, nor be a part of, and thus, I was sent away. I am quite contented to walk alone for a few moments."

"I – I should be glad to accompany you," Robert found himself saying, an urge to walk with the lady who had invaded his thoughts for so long growing within his heart. "Even if it is only a short distance, I –"

"But you would be seen walking with a companion."

The slight sharpness to her words had his face burning with embarrassment over his past behaviors.

"I do not think any less of you, Miss Gregory."

"No?"

Again came that touch of disbelief in her words, the

suspected awareness that she was, in his eyes, a good deal lesser than he.

Robert closed his eyes, letting out an exclamation of exasperation that he had not intended to reveal to her. It was only when he caught her looking at him sidelong that his embarrassment began to grow and, as the silence blossomed between them while Robert still found his steps following alongside hers, he felt the need to say something.

He saw Miss Gregory's frown and then let out a sigh of frustration.

"Forgive me, Miss Gregory. I ought not to be continually walking with you when you have stated that you have no need for company. However, please be assured that I should very much like to walk with you for a time."

Miss Gregory's eyes narrowed slightly as she studied him as if searching for the truth in his expression.

"I am now required to wait for my aunt since if I were to turn this corner, I would not be in her view," she said, turning and glancing behind her, to where Lady Langdon stood chattering happily with a lady who Robert was not acquainted with himself. Miss Gregory's eyes caught his again. "Were you walking alone this afternoon?"

"I was in company with Lord Venables. However, after a prolonged conversation, I begged of him to take his leave."

Miss Gregory looked at him sharply and he shook his head in answer to her unspoken question.

"We did not argue, no. It is only that I have had my thoughts a little disordered of late and Lord Venables thought to share his particular opinions also." A small, sad smile tugged at his mouth as he glanced at her before looking away. "It is difficult when one questions one's character."

Seeing the flash of awareness in her eyes, Robert

looked away, now wishing that he had not said anything at all. She did not need to know and, most likely, did not wish to know, his weaknesses, and his failures. Whyever had he thought it a wise idea to share such a thing with her?

"I am sorry for that." Her response surprised him and he saw her smile gently, as a flyaway brown curl brushed across her forehead. "To struggle with one's thoughts can be very trying. Lord Venables is a good friend to you, however, I assume?"

"Our parting is only for the moment," Robert replied, quickly. "I am sure that we will be in conversation again very soon."

"Might I speak openly, Lord Crampton?" He looked back at her quickly, seeing the steadiness in her eyes and finding himself less than inclined to agree for her to do so. He was not quite certain that he had enough fortitude to hear yet more criticism of his character, but Miss Gregory continued on, speaking to him regardless of his response. "It seems that you are a gentleman who is aware of his faults but does not wish to address them."

He blinked.

"I beg your pardon?"

"You knew that to speak to me in such a dismissive manner when my aunt and I came to call was hurtful. However, you did not apologize to me at the time and, in fact, only chose to do so when my aunt was gone from your presence."

The truth in her words rendered Robert so uncomfortable that he could not keep hold of her gaze, turning his head away as if to see what Lady Langdon was doing at present. Clearing his throat, he spread his hands.

"You are suggesting, Miss Gregory, that I have a

prideful character which does not like to do anything or say anything that might injure it."

She tilted her head.

"That may be so, yes. Although I have heard that all gentlemen are somewhat arrogant."

He dropped his head.

I do not want her to see such a thing in me.

The fierceness of such a thought rushed through him and he caught his breath, lifting his head to speak to her again, to tell her that his thoughts were so very conflicted but that he hoped that any flaws, such as the ones she saw in him, might soon be changed.

Alas, he was too late. She spoke again before he could.

"Ah, and now my aunt is beckoning me to return to her. It seems that she has need of her companion once more." Miss Gregory gave him a small smile which Robert struggled to return, embarrassed that, as yet, he had not been able to return a single word to her. "Good afternoon, Lord Crampton."

"Miss Gregory."

To Robert's increased mortification, his hand had shot out – seemingly of its own accord – and caught Miss Gregory's arm. He could see the astonishment in her eyes as she looked down at where he had caught her, the pink that came into her cheeks as she then looked up into his face, and the slight lifting of her brows.

Robert dropped his hand and placed it behind his back, fastening it to the other for fear that he might do something all the more ridiculous.

"Yes, Lord Crampton, was there something else?"

Why did I prevent her from leaving?

Robert searched wildly for a reason to have her stay, for an explanation for why he had said her name and pulled her back and slowly, so very, very slowly, the truth began to reveal itself to him.

"I should like to speak to you again, Miss Gregory."

Her green eyes flared.

"I beg your pardon?"

"I know that I must seem rather foolish, Miss Gregory, but you are the only young lady of my acquaintance who seems willing to speak to me with any sort of honesty."

A teasing smile pulled at her lips although Robert could see how she fought to keep her expression calm.

"But you dislike being spoken to in such a manner, Lord Crampton. It clearly causes you great consternation."

His rueful smile spread across his face.

"Indeed, that is so," he said heavily, feeling all the more discomposed but yet determined to find a way to speak to Miss Gregory again despite such a feeling. "The truth is, Miss Gregory, I cannot understand nor explain such a desire, but it is there nonetheless," he replied, as the lady's smile faded, and her eyes became watchful. "Lord Venables will further our conversation too, I am sure, and I should like to speak to you again as well."

She tilted her head, her eyes narrowing.

"But I am not to be considered anything near to your equal, Lord Crampton," she said, as a pinch of color came into both cheeks. "I am only a companion. Society thinks less of me because of my situation. You yourself have thought so also, have you not?"

Robert knew that he could not deny this and spread his hands wide.

"My judgment has been poor," he told her, frankly. "I *have* thought your manner and your freedom of speaking to me to be quite rude and improper, I will not lie about that." Miss Gregory's eyes flickered but she said nothing in response. "After our first meeting, I told myself that a companion ought to treat someone such as myself with more respect – that I *deserved* that from you – but my opinion on that has slowly begun to change."

"Oh?"

"I have been wrong in my consideration of you, and in my actions, Miss Gregory. I will again beg for your forgiveness. Your words are honest, and they are painful to me, but I am slowly becoming grateful for them. I wish to speak with you again for fear that the gentleman I am at present is not the gentleman I ought to be." He ran one hand over his eyes, wanting to quell the stream of words that flowed from his lips. "There is more to my story than I have revealed to you, also. There are reasons behind my eagerness for the *ton* to think well of me, reasons that I am only just considering. The weight of my thoughts is binding my mind and bringing a despondency to my soul, yet I do not turn from it. I will not shy away from whatever you have to say, I assure you."

Miss Gregory drew in a deep breath and then let it out slowly, carefully considering. And then, she spoke.

"Tell me something, Lord Crampton – and you must be truthful with me, I beg of you."

He spread his hands.

"Of course."

"Is what happened in the carriage a few days ago just as you said?"

A frown pulled at his brows.

"You mean when you and your aunt discovered me?"

He was very relieved that no whispers had spread through the *ton* about his difficult evening and cursed himself silently for not, as yet, thanking Miss Gregory for keeping silent.

"Yes, that is what I mean."

Robert nodded, spreading his hands.

"It is exactly as I said, Miss Gregory," he promised, praying that, somehow, she would see the truth in his eyes. "I have not told you a lie."

She considered this for a few moments, looking back at him carefully, her eyes searching his face as her lips pursed gently.

Then, she smiled.

"I shall be glad to talk with you again, whenever you wish it, Lord Crampton, if you are truly willing to speak to a mere companion," she said, bringing forth a great wave of relief into Robert's heart as he saw the twinkle in her eye. "Even though I feel that I should warn you that you will not, most likely, be glad to hear what I say."

"I shall do my best to endeavor not to react in a poor fashion," he promised, as she nodded, spreading out one hand towards her aunt. "And now, I have kept you for too long. I do pray that your aunt will not berate you for your tardiness, which was entirely my doing. Good afternoon, Miss Gregory."

Her smile was a genuine one and, despite his confusion over his own desires and expectations, Robert smiled back.

"Good afternoon, Lord Crampton," she murmured, before turning away and returning to Lady Langdon.

CHAPTER EIGHT

"I am astonished."

Honora laughed.

"As was I, I confess it," she replied, as Lady Albina stared back at her with wide eyes. "I did not think that he would ever wish to be in my company again after I spoke to him so sharply at his townhouse!"

Lady Albina shook her head in seeming disbelief, whilst Honora herself merely smiled and considered, yet again, what it was that Lord Crampton wanted by such an association. There was, she knew, no delight on his part when it came to her frankness but yet, for whatever reason, he appeared to want to talk to her again regardless.

"You say that he had been walking with Lord Venables?"

"He stated that he had asked his friend to step away for a time, for I believe Lord Venables was being rather forthright and Lord Crampton had, therefore, a good deal to think on," Honora replied, shrugging one shoulder and, at the same time, glancing all around her for fear of being overheard.

Lady Albina nodded slowly, tilting her head to one side, her eyes searching Honora's.

"Then he may have been feeling a little... confused?"

"Vulnerable," Honora agreed, as her friend continued to watch her carefully. "You do not think me foolish to have agreed to converse with him again?"

"No, indeed not!" Lady Albina replied hastily, although her eyes remained thoughtful. "It is only that you had such a strong dislike for him after your first meeting, I am surprised to hear that you now intend to return to his company willingly!"

Honora pressed her lips together, deciding that she would not reveal all that she felt for Lord Crampton to her friend. There was an interest in him, certainly, but there was also an increasing desire for his company which, as yet, she was uncertain of.

"I suppose I am curious to see what it is that he wishes to talk about," she replied, a rueful smile on her face. "He stated that there is more to his situation and circumstances than I know at present. He also told me that there were reasons behind his eagerness for the *ton* to think well of him – reasons that, I presume, he wishes to share with me, although I do not know why I am to be so favored." She shrugged as Lady Albina smiled. "I have not informed my aunt of his request nor of my agreement, for fear that she would become greatly upset and state that it is not my place to do so."

"That may be wise, although I must hope that you know of *my* high opinion of you. I believe that you will speak well to Lord Crampton no matter what the subject at hand is."

Honora smiled her thanks at the compliment and then decided to change the subject of their conversation, finding herself quite worn out when it came to talking of Lord

Crampton. He had been occupying her thoughts a good deal, ever since the night they had found him on the cobbles beside his carriage and, even now, four days later, she was struggling to think of anything other than him.

It was a very strange state of affairs. To have found Lord Crampton so injured was one thing, but to then hear that another person had brought about that injury was quite another! On top of which, she had found herself angry with him for his hope that, in having them visit, they would not speak ill of him to any other rather than thinking only to thank them. That conversation and visit had ended in a rather strange, troubling manner and Honora had been all the more conflicted when she had stumbled across him in the park and, whilst she had not found their conversation particularly enjoyable, his last request – and the explanation which had followed – had been more than a little curious. Thus, Honora had found herself thinking of the fellow all the more, wondering what it was that he had meant in asking her to talk with him again and, even now, thinking about the strange confusion in his eyes when he had spoken of Lord Venables.

"Good evening, Lady Albina."

Honora turned her head, seeing a gentleman drawing close to them, although his eyes were set upon Lady Albina. He was very tall indeed, almost towering over Lady Albina, although he had a thin frame that diminished any hint of an intimidating appearance. As Honora glanced at her friend, she was surprised to see the gentle blossoming pink in the lady's cheeks – and quickly realized that this person was of interest to Lady Albina. She dropped her head and took a step back nearer to the shadows in the room, knowing that, as a companion, she would not be introduced to a gentleman. Her aunt was dancing at this present moment, else Honora would have made her way back to her without hesitation but, for the time being, she simply stood quietly at the edge of the room.

"Good evening, Lord Kingston," she heard Lady Albina say, seeing how her friend fixed her gaze to the gentleman. "How very good to see you returned to London."

"You were my first thought," he told her, making Honora smile softly.

Lord Kingston was clearly eager to press as many compliments as he could upon Lady Albina. This comment, however, seemed to unsettle Lady Albina, who immediately turned around in an attempt to find Honora, her cheeks now very red indeed.

"Lord Kingston, might I present my friend, Miss Honora Gregory?" she said quickly, as Honora was beckoned forward. A little uncertain, Honora came back to stand beside Lady Albina, then dropped her head and curtsied. "Miss Gregory, this is the Earl of Kingston."

"Very nice to meet you," came the jovial reply, as he gave Honora a swift bow although, she noted, his eyes immediately returned to Lady Albina. "I do hope that you will not mind if I steal Lady Albina away, Miss Gregory? I have heard that the next set is about to start, and I should *very* much like to step out to dance with you."

This last sentence was directed towards Lady Albina who, with a brilliant smile and not even a glance towards Honora, accepted in an instant. Honora watched as Lady Albina settled her hand on Lord Kingston's arm and stepped away, leaving Honora to return to her place by the edge of the room as the rest of the guests moved and conversed around her.

She sighed, wondering if she would ever have cause to have such a blush fill her cheeks, or her eyes to sparkle with such an interest in the gentleman before her that she could do nothing other than look up into his face and forget about those around her entirely.

You already know the answer to such dreams, she told herself sternly, afraid that she would get quite lost in such a fantasy if she permitted it. *You are a companion to your aunt. She is the one searching for a match, not you. You can offer nothing to any gentleman, save for your smiles.*

Telling herself that she ought not to be thinking of affection, or desire, or the like for it would only pain her heart, Honora lifted her chin, shook her head gently to disperse the many thoughts contained within it, and then looked out across the crowd.

The soiree this evening was a large one. Lord Hastings had made certain to invite as many guests as he could fit into his house and had opened up his drawing-room, his music room, library, and parlor for them all. Honora knew that dancing was taking place in the music room and half thought about going in search of her aunt, only to notice something rather curious.

A footman was standing to one side of the room, looking out across it with such a sharpness in his gaze that Honora was taken aback. Normally, a footman would keep his eyes lowered and, should he be required to lift his head, would not look directly at the guests, but this one was not in any way so reserved. He was looking at each person individually, although his eyes flicked over Honora rather than give her any particular attention. Honora studied him a little more, taking in the small silver tray that he held which, much to her bewilderment, had only one glass upon it.

How very strange, Honora thought, wondering what the

footman was doing by behaving so – and if Lord Hastings knew of it. She was about to make her way across the room to see if she could watch him a little more closely, only for a voice to catch her attention.

"You are standing alone, Miss Gregory."

Her skin prickled and, much to her surprise, a smile pulled at her lips at the sound of Lord Crampton's voice although, at the same time, a tension began to writhe through her veins.

"I am, Lord Crampton, just as I ought.". Turning her attention to him, she saw him bow, took in the pinched look in his expression and, thereafter, dropped into a quick curtsey of her own. "I hope that you are recovered?"

Perhaps he too feels a slight awkwardness over our previous conversation.

"I thank you." His smile was a little warmer, lighting his expression. "My back is a little pained, but I was determined not to linger at home any longer. I have endured enough dull evenings or short walks in the park!"

Honora's smile was a genuine one.

"I am glad of it. I am sure society has missed you."

His smile was a little twisted.

"Mayhap."

One quick glance around the room told her that there were at least three young ladies looking towards them. A small flush of heat began to spiral up into her chest, rendering her cheeks rather warm.

"I am sure, Lord Crampton, that you have been missed. A few young ladies in particular are watching our conversation, wondering, no doubt, why it is that a gentleman is speaking to a companion at such length."

Lord Crampton's eyes flared but, to her surprise, he did

not allow his gaze to rove around the room as she had expected.

"I am quite contented here, Miss Gregory."

"That astonishes me a great deal, Lord Crampton." Her usual honesty was again coming to the fore, and she spoke without giving much thought to her words. "Have you no intentions to pursue one of them?"

This seemed to confuse Lord Crampton a great deal, for he frowned heavily, his brows low over his eyes, and a deep groove forming between them. He did not answer her immediately but rather simply looked back at her, studying her as though he did not understand her question.

"It is a strange thing – and, in fact, an unusual thing – for a young lady to ask, Miss Gregory," he said, quietly, and the flush in Honora's cheeks deepened. She noted silently that he had referred to her as a young lady and not as a companion, finding a gentle warmth lifting her heart for a moment as she responded.

"You know that you can expect such conversation from me, do you not?" she asked, lifting one eyebrow gently. I suppose I am a little surprised, given what I have seen of your previous behavior."

Lord Crampton frowned and he cleared his throat gruffly, perhaps displeased with being reminded of what had gone before.

"I have no thought of pursuing matrimony at present."

"I see." Her smile softened. "These young ladies who gaze at you with such eager hope in their eyes are to be disappointed, then."

He dropped his head.

"I fear that you and Lord Venables are in partnership together, Miss Gregory, given that you are both eager to speak to me about the same matter."

She did not know what to say nor how to respond. What had begun as an uncomfortable awareness that the young ladies in the room were watching them had now ended as a conversation about matrimony and her confusing delight over the fact that he was not intending to wed any of them. Clasping her hands loosely in front of her, Honora attempted to separate the whirling emotions that flew about her heart, but somehow only managed to add to her confusion. "My Lord."

Lord Crampton still had not answered her, and a footman chose that very moment to draw near, bringing Lord Crampton a glass of what looked like whisky or brandy. She sighed inwardly and turned her head away, only to then see that the footman she had been watching, the one who had behaved very oddly, was now no longer able to be seen.

Her stomach twisted. She looked back at Lord Crampton, seeing him lift his glass to his lips and, given the way that he was gripping the glass so tightly, fearing that he would throw it back in one swallow. The footman who had offered Lord Crampton the drink had departed without even looking towards her, without even thinking that she too might like something to drink – and a warning rang through Honora's mind. She had no thought other than to take the drink from Lord Crampton's hand – but it appeared she was a little too late.

"Wait!" Her hand shot out, pulling at his wrist. Brandy spilled from it, with some spurting from his mouth which Honora only just managed to step away from. The glass tumbled to the floor, shattering as it did so and drawing the attention of almost every person in the room.

Honora's face flamed.

"Whatever are you doing?" Lord Crampton spluttered,

pulling out a handkerchief and wiping it across his face, clearly mortified. "Miss Gregory, I –"

A sudden commotion caught both of their attention, making Honora turn her head and Lord Crampton's complaints come to a sudden end. The Duke and Duchess of Strathaven came into the room, their daughter behind them, and in that instant, everyone turned their attention away from Honora and Lord Crampton and instead looked towards their honored guests.

"Miss Gregory, that was a deliberate act!" Lord Crampton sounded offended, his eyes wide and a faint spot of color coming into each cheek.

"Well, yes, it was, but it is not for the reasons that you think," Honora said hurriedly, glancing down at her gown and running her fingers across her skirts, relieved that she had no splashes of brandy on them. "You see, only a few minutes ago –"

"You saw the Duke and Duchess of Strathaven arriving and thought to embarrass me in front of them!"

Lord Crampton's exclamation shocked Honora to the core. She stared at him with wide eyes, her heart beating furiously as an ice-cold hand began to grasp it.

"I have done no such thing," she whispered, unable to put any strength into her voice such was her shock. "I was attempting to help you."

His lip curled, and his blue eyes darkened to the inky blackness of a night sky. In a moment, he had changed completely, believing her to be capable of deliberate cruelty.

"In an effort to push through the arrogance you have so clearly seen in me, you thought to do such a thing just as the Duke arrived for fear that your words would not be enough!" Shaking his head, Lord Crampton's jaw clenched, his fury burning Honora's skin. "Miss Gregory, I may be stubborn and prideful, but I was eager to pay attention to your thoughts and opinions. You did not need to go to such an extreme!"

Tears threatened, but Honora blinked them away in an instant, knowing that they came from a place of anger rather than upset.

"I have done nothing of the sort, Lord Crampton," she stated, finally able to find strength in her voice. "If you would permit me even a *moment* to explain, then you might realize that it is not as you think."

Lord Crampton's eyes flashed, but he remained silent. Honora steeled herself, her hands tight, her fingernails biting into the soft skin of her palms.

"The drink that you were given," she said, as Lord Crampton continued to mop his face with the handkerchief, muttering as he did so. "I was sure that – Lord Crampton!"

She could not finish her sentence for, at the very next moment, Lord Crampton dropped his handkerchief, staggered forward, and pressed both hands to his head. A loud groan emitted from his mouth as he fell into Honora, who struggled to catch him. Much to her relief, a footman stepped forward to help, and then another, until, finally, Lord Crampton was sitting in a chair – albeit bent forward with his head in his hands and his elbows resting on his knees. The anger and the upset that she felt was gone in an instant, replaced now with naught but concern.

"Lord Crampton." She bent down, looking up into his face, just as a few of the guests began to realize what had happened. "Are you well?"

Honora knew that she ought to step away, ought to leave Lord Crampton alone so that she would not be seen, given that a companion's priority was their charge and, thereafter, to remain as hidden and as invisible as possible.

Her aunt would not be pleased should she discover her in such a position

"I feel..."

Another small groan came from his lips as if he was unable to form any more words by which to answer her.

"I think Lord Crampton will need to return home," Lord Hastings said, making Honora jerk in surprise as she turned her head to see the host looking down at Lord Crampton with concern. "I will have the carriage brought and have one of my staff fetch the physician. You will be better at home, Crampton, I am sure."

Honora made to rise, only for Lord Crampton's hand to reach out and take hers. Her breath hitched as she looked into his face, seeing the pallor of his cheeks and his bloodshot eyes. The man was clearly unwell. Her eyes closed for a moment, her stomach twisting. She had reacted instinctively with the glass of brandy, and it seemed that she had been right to do so, regardless of the scene it had caused. Her heart quailed at the thought of what Lord Crampton's situation might now be, had he drunk all of it.

"I am sorry." Lord Crampton's voice was low and rasping, each word seeming to be an effort. His fingers clasped hers tightly, however, and the fierceness in his gaze surprised her, given the fact that he was so clearly unwell. "I was wrong."

"Yes," she answered, unequivocally. "You were. But you must rest and recover. I do hope that the physician will be able to help you."

He grimaced, made to say something more, only to drop his head and groan again. Honora rose to her feet, pulling her hand from Lord Crampton's for fear that someone would see, relieved when she turned around that the guests were still very much enthralled with the Duke's arrival, rather than paying much attention to Lord Crampton. Even with Lord Hastings' involvement, it seemed that the Duke and Duchess of Strathaven caught everyone's interest. Her aunt was nowhere to be seen.

"Whatever happened?"

Lady Albina was by her elbow at the next moment, with Lord Kingston only a step or two behind. Her eyes were wide as she looked to Lord Crampton, just as the footmen came to help him rise, intending to lead him to the door.

"He was taken very unwell," Honora replied, as Lady Albina let out a small exclamation of surprise at just how weak Lord Crampton seemed to be. Honora too felt her concern grow, for Lord Crampton now had two footmen assisting him, with one on either side, supporting him heavily. Whatever he had imbibed, it had clearly had a very pronounced effect. "I do hope he will recover very soon."

She did not want to tell her friend the truth of her suspicions, not yet. There was no proof that what she suspected was true.

"Indeed, he looks very ill," Lady Albina said, shaking her head. "Ah, but look! The Duke and Duchess of Strathaven have arrived! I had heard whispers that they would be in attendance, but I did not know for certain!"

Honora's attention was then pulled towards the as yet unknown Duke, although her mind and heart still lingered on Lord Crampton. She could not forget what he had said to her, could not set aside what he had accused her of, but yet her concern for him and her confusion over what she had seen seemed to overcome both of the former. Just what had been in the glass? And why had the footman been waiting to give that glass to Lord Crampton specifically? Honora was sure that it would not have been done by his own volition but rather on the instructions of someone else – but she had not even the smallest imagining as to who such a person might be, nor why they would wish to harm Lord Crampton.

"Then he was telling the truth," she murmured to herself, realizing that there could not be any doubt about what Lord Crampton had previously told her about his fall from the carriage. She was now convinced that someone, for whatever reason, was attempting to hurt Lord Crampton in a violent way – she just had to wonder whether Lord Crampton himself was aware of it.

"Did you say something?"

Honora caught herself, turning to Lady Albina with a quick smile.

"No, nothing of importance," she said, trying to set the matter aside. "Now, if you are acquainted with the Duke and Duchess, why do you not greet them? I shall be quite contented to stand here and wait for you."

Lady Albina shook her head, reaching out to press Honora's hand.

"You ought to be permitted to be introduced to the Duke, since you are, in fact, a Lady," she said, firmly. "Why do you not speak to your aunt?"

Honora sighed, aware of Lady Albina's gentle encouragements but finding the idea preposterous.

"Because my aunt is fixed solely on her own situation and believes that no gentleman would ever consider me. She thinks she is giving me a great encouragement in bringing me here as a companion, although she does expect me to behave just as she demands." A small, sad laugh escaped her, and Honora shook her head, looking past Lady Albina to where the Duke and Duchess of Strathaven were smiling and laughing with the guests who surrounded them. "That will never be me."

"Then you resign yourself to this role." The hardness of Lady Albina's words caught Honora off guard, and she looked back at her friend with wide eyes. "If you will not be courageous, if you will not fight for an opportunity to be a lady instead of a companion, then you cannot cry about whatever situation you find yourself in." Honora opened her mouth, but Lady Albina stepped forward, grasped both of Honora's hands in hers, and leaned close, her eyes meeting Honora's. "Be brave and bold, Honora," she said, firmly. "Speak to your aunt. Demand a change in your circumstances. Speak frankly, just as you have done with Lord Crampton, and see what may come of it." She smiled but the steel in her eyes spoke of a determination which, as yet, Honora did not feel. "Then you will know, at the very least, that you did all you could."

Honora closed her eyes, finding herself recoiling from the idea but, at the same time, recognizing the truth in Lady Albina's words.

"Would any gentleman even wish to speak with me, dance with me?" she asked, her voice quavering as she kept her eyes closed. "The *ton* knows of my situation. My aunt has made sure of that."

"Yes, of course they would. Lord Crampton, I know, would be more than eager to, should he be given the opportunity, since he has so clearly sought you out in amongst the *ton*." There was a confidence in Lady Albina's voice that had Honora opening her eyes, letting out a long breath as she did so. "I am *certain* that you would not be left feeling ashamed, Miss Gregory. Instead, you would have hope and, mayhap, even a future husband already seeking you out."

Honora tried to speak, but the words would not come.

Lady Albina had set out a small, flickering hope and now Honora could not help but cling to it. She could only nod, seeing the way that her friend's eyes flared and seeing the bright, excited smile which spread across her face.

It was time now to be bold.

CHAPTER NINE

Robert gazed disinterestedly down at his plate. He had no appetite and yet knew that it would be best for him to eat something if he wanted to regain even a little of his strength.

"My Lord?"

He looked up, to see his butler already at the door.

"Lord Venables has come to call."

There was no eagerness in Robert's heart to see his friend, but he nodded regardless. His mind was swirling with thoughts but mayhap it would be good to share them with another.

"Very well," he said, heaving a sigh. "Bring... something else for us to eat."

He shook his head down at his plate, as though the food itself were at fault for refusing to be appetizing enough for him to enjoy.

The butler nodded and left the room without a word, returning just as silently only a few moments later with Lord Venables. Robert had expected to see a frown upon the man's face or, at the very least, a grimace, but he was astonished to see Lord Venables' eyes wide with concern and his lips pursed as he strode into the room.

"You are unwell."

"I have *been* unwell," Robert corrected, not yet rising from his chair, but gesturing to Lord Venables to join him at the dining table. "Forgive me for not removing to the drawing-room or the parlor – I have not yet broken my fast today... although I have not found myself eager to do so either."

"I heard it all," Lord Venables murmured, sitting down quickly although his gaze was still on Robert. "You were taken ill at Lord Hastings' soiree?"

"I was." Robert hesitated, not certain whether to tell Lord Venables everything but, eventually, choosing to do so. "Someone made sure that I was, deliberately."

"This was done to you on purpose?" Lord Venables did not sound disbelieving, much to Robert's relief, but there was a small degree of skepticism in his eyes. "Why?"

Robert spread his hands.

"I do not know," he replied, quietly. "You need not believe me, for it does sound quite ridiculous, but I am sure of it now."

The maids brought in a tray of cakes and another with coffee and china cups, setting them down before Robert and Lord Venables but, eyeing them, Robert found still that his appetite was not at all whetted.

"The accident with the carriage," he began, as Lord Venables quickly reached for a slice of fruit cake, clearly a little hungry. "That was done purposefully, with the sole aim of injuring me. This illness has been brought on by something which I was given – although I am relieved that I did not drink all of it."

His lips turned upwards as he thought of Miss Gregory who had reacted so swiftly, and with such purpose that he had been unable to throw back his drink as he had intended. The very next moment, that smile was wiped from his face as he recalled how he had thrown recriminations at her, and the shock on her face as he had said it.

He was thoroughly ashamed of himself.

"You will have to explain this from the beginning," Lord Venables stated, firmly. "Every detail. I must know precisely what took place if I am to believe you."

Taking in a deep breath, Robert set his shoulders and began to explain. Lord Venables listened without a word, although when Robert reached the part where Miss Gregory had thrown out a hand and knocked the glass away from his mouth, Lord Venables' eyes widened with surprise, his brows lifting.

"She is a courageous young lady," he said – a statement which Robert could not disagree with. "To have done such a thing without hesitation and going solely on her own instinct..." he shook his head, "that could have had severe consequences, should you have been quite well."

Robert had not thought of such a thing before. Grimacing, he dropped his head into his hands, feeling all the more embarrassed that he had behaved in such a way.

"I spoke very harshly to her," he said, gruffly, hating to admit to such a thing, but finding the urge to do so growing steadily. "I ought not to have done, I know, but I did."

"In what way?" Lord Venables asked, picking up a cup and pouring some coffee into it, before doing the same for Robert. "Did you say something to her you ought not to have done?"

The urge to keep the details to himself prevented Robert from replying for a few moments, as he struggled against his pride. Seeing his friend's lifted eyebrow, he let out a heavy sigh.

"If you must know," he said, with as much dignity as possible, "When Miss Gregory knocked the glass from my hand, the brandy went everywhere, including on my face, neck, and clothing, and did so just as the Duke and Duchess of Strathaven came into the room."

A growing awareness came into Lord Venables' eyes, just as a wave of heat from the embarrassment began to spread up Robert's neck.

"I accused her of doing so purposefully so that I would be belittled and embarrassed in front of the Duke."

"I see," Lord Venables murmured, no judgment in his eyes or expression, but rather a calm acceptance, as though he had expected as much from Robert. "I do hope that you have apologized to her?"

"I attempted to do so but, being as ill as I was, found it rather difficult," he admitted, at which Lord Venables nodded in understanding. "I will have to do so again, of course. But whether or not she will forgive me or even *tolerate* my company after this, I cannot say. Indeed, I would not be surprised if she did not wish to speak to me again, and certainly, I would not blame her for it. She is the most extraordinary creature and I behaved appallingly.

"Miss Gregory is an extraordinary young lady," Lord Venables agreed swiftly. "Especially given that she was the one to recognize that there was something wrong with your brandy." His lips twisted, pulling to one side for a moment. "Did she say how she became aware of such a thing?"

"No, she did not," Robert replied, frowning as he realized that he had given no thought to how Miss Gregory had been aware of what was in his brandy. "I will have to ask her, of course. Being a companion, I suppose, has its benefits. She would have been simply standing and watching the comings and goings of the guests."

Lord Venables chuckled, a brightness in his eyes that seemed to lift the darkness from their present discussion.

"It is a little mirthful that the one lady who initially did not want to be in your company is the one who has now *twice* been present when you have been entirely discomposed!" he said, making Robert smile ruefully. "Recently it appears as though she has been a little more in your company, however…"

Robert hesitated, the look on Miss Gregory's face as he had snarled at her floating in his mind.

"I would not be surprised if she wanted nothing more to do with me now," he replied, heavily. "I now have the grace at least to state that I was very foolish to speak to her as I did that first evening. I look back upon my behavior and see my arrogance and my pridefulness in a way that I have never done before."

"If anything, Miss Gregory seems to be a very forgiving sort," Lord Venables said, picking up his coffee to sip. "A rare creature, I think. I do not think that she ought to be a companion. I have heard of her father's situation, and it does not appear to be any of his own doing. The crops have failed due to the weather, due to flooding, and he has been forced to do all manner of things to attempt to save his lands. Miss Gregory should be here to make a normal come out into society, not as a companion to that ridiculous aunt of hers."

He eyed Robert speculatively, but Robert did not say anything, either in agreement or otherwise. He was silently thinking of the lady, recalling their first introduction and how neither of them had really wanted to be in conversation or company with the other. He had been sure that she had an acrid tongue and an unforgiving, unrelenting spirit, but now that he knew her a little better, Robert was eager for her company. The thought of their acquaintance ending solely because of his own poor behavior was a painful thought indeed, bringing such a stab of pain to his soul that he absently rubbed his chest with one hand. Yes, he agreed wholeheartedly that she ought not to be a companion. Her father might well be impoverished, but that did not detract from the loveliness of the lady herself – although her lack of dowry would turn away many a gentleman.

Would it turn you away?

Robert cleared his throat and reached for his coffee, trying to shake away that last thought. Lord Venables was correct, of course, he *would* have to speak to Miss Gregory again and hear what she had to say about what had taken place. How had she known what was in his glass? And would he be able to find the words to express not only his great regret about speaking to her as he had done, but to admit to her that he had done so simply because of his pride? That he had reflected on his words to her and found not only those but his manner towards her utterly intolerable. The thought burned in his mind and Robert dropped his head, knowing that such a conversation would be painful indeed but yet, for her, Robert knew he would do it.

~

"Good afternoon, Miss Gregory."

She smiled at him, and a pang of guilt stabbed into Robert's heart. He did not deserve such kindness from her.

"Thank you for agreeing to walk with me," he said, as her aunt stood behind her, having only just emerged from the carriage. "Thank you also, Lady Langdon."

Lady Langdon sniffed and turned her eyes away, her dislike of him clear.

"It is most unusual for a gentleman to insist that he walk with my *companion* for a short while, Lord Crampton," she told him, her voice high pitched and her frame tight. "If you had not sent four letters, one after the other, I doubt I would have agreed. It is just as well, I suppose, that the park is quiet this afternoon."

Robert's stomach twisted as Miss Gregory immediately dropped her head, her smile broken in an instant. He did not like the way that her aunt spoke of her, did not like the way in which she was continually reminded of her position, nor how unusual and strange it was for a gentleman to be eager to walk with her.

"I confess that I do not see Miss Gregory as a companion, Lady Langdon," he said quietly, his words bringing Miss Gregory's head up in an instant, her green eyes rounding. "I see her for what she is – a young lady of society who has done me a great service."

Lady Langdon turned her eyes towards him for a moment, a flicker of confusion in them as she held his gaze before muttering something and turning her head away again.

"Shall we walk?" Miss Gregory asked, breaking the tension that Robert was beginning to feel between himself and Lady Langdon. "It is a very warm day, and it might be agreeable to find some shade."

"But of course."

Inwardly hesitating, Robert took a breath and then

offered her his arm, all the more surprised when she accepted it without question. A tightness in his throat meant that he could not speak for a few moments as they began to walk together, and he struggled to find the right thing to say so that they might begin their conversation.

"You are recovered, I hope?"

Glancing down at her, Robert tried to smile.

"Yes, much recovered," he replied, glad that the weakness and chills had now left his frame, although he was still struggling with his appetite. "I did want to speak to you about what took place that night, Miss Gregory. It seems that I was taken ill shortly after I drank the glass of brandy."

"Yes, indeed, it was as I expected!" Miss Gregory exclaimed, making Robert's eyes flare wide. "The brandy had something in it that ought not to have been there."

Pressing his lips together tightly for a moment to keep back any further questions that sprang to his lips, Robert glanced down at her again. He wanted to express his apology to her first, before they began to discuss anything else.

"Miss Gregory, I did you a great wrong," he said, finding each word difficult as it burned up his throat and seared his lips. "I spoke harshly and laid things at your door which held no truth and for that, I know I must apologize."

She tipped her head gently, looking up at him with eyes which were swirling with various questions and, he considered, differing emotions. He did not know what else to say, waiting for her to speak, waiting for her to say something in answer to his statement.

"You greatly offended me, Lord Crampton." Her words offered him no comfort, burning a hole in his heart, and making his shame increase all the more. It was a disconcerting and unsettling experience and not one which Robert appreciated. "You may not know my character particularly well, but I can assure you that I am not a cruel sort," she continued, quietly. "I would never do such a thing as that. I might believe that your connection with the Duke of Strathaven poses various difficulties, but I certainly would never attempt to embarrass you in front of him. That would be cruel indeed."

"I can see now that I was wrong," he told her, wanting to rid himself of this feeling of guilt which continued to blossom within his heart, as though it loved resting there and disconcerting him so. "I should not even have entertained the thought. I can only give you my sincere apology, Miss Gregory. To have even *thought* such a thing was deeply wrong."

The wind blew gently between them, chasing Miss Gregory's curls which danced about her temples as she continued to look up at him, trusting him to lead her along the path without difficulty. Robert found it hard to return her gaze, all too aware that all the guilt and shame he felt had not immediately evaporated the moment that he had apologized.

That is because there is more to say.

"I accept your apology, my Lord," she murmured, softly. "It is honestly given, and I cannot withhold my forgiveness." Her lips pulled into a gentle smile although that smile then faded almost immediately. "I must hope that you will be able to meet with the Duke and Duchess of Strathaven again very soon. I am sure that they will be glad to reacquaint themselves with you."

Her tone had dulled, and Robert frowned, not quite sure what to say.

"That – that is not a connection that I am considering at present." He cleared his throat, choosing to speak openly about what was within his heart. "My character is greatly flawed in your eyes, is it not?"

Miss Gregory looked surprised, her brows lifting and her eyes a little wider than before.

"Do you wish me to be truthful?"

He held out his free hand in front of him, palm upwards.

"Please."

"Do you not already know?" A small smile pulled at one corner of her mouth, her eyes twinkling. "I am sure that I have stated it outright before - and that you did not much appreciate me doing so."

He shrugged.

"Then I was a fool," he replied, making her laugh. "Miss Gregory, you are the only lady in all of London who does not smile and laugh and delight in every aspect of my company. I should, by rights, be less than inclined towards you, and yet I find myself desiring entirely the opposite."

"And so you are still here, asking me to tell you about the defect I see in your character," she said, softly. "You know full well, Lord Crampton, that I have seen pride and arrogance in both your manner and conversation. That is not to say that you have no other qualities, but rather that these are the things which came to the fore at our first meeting, and I cannot help but surmise that they come simply because of your connection with the Duke."

It was, for whatever reason, satisfying to hear her say it all so clearly. There came no anger nor upset to his heart but, instead, a small, steady calmness that quietened his spirits rather than sent them into an uproar.

He was not going to dismiss what Miss Gregory had said to him. No, he was going to allow it to rest in his heart and in his thoughts, so that it might pervade him and, perhaps, change his character more to that of someone whom Miss Gregory might think a good deal better of.

Why do you want her to have a better impression of your character?

"I have not upset you, I hope?"

The tentativeness in her voice made him look down at her sharply, only to then quickly force a smile so that the anxiety in her eyes would fade.

"No, not at all," he promised. "I asked you to be truthful, Miss Gregory, and you have been so. I cannot be angry about that." His expression relaxed, his smile becoming natural rather than forced. "I did inform you that there was more to my story than you know – although mayhap you do not wish to know it." Taking in a deep breath, he continued to speak in that honest vein that was so unfamiliar to him. "My father was a merchant – the third son of the third son of a previous Earl of Crampton, so far removed from the nobility of today. My mother was a seamstress. We did not have any great claims and I lived my life with the expectation of following in my father's footsteps – and for a time, I did. I worked alongside him, only to be informed that I was now to take on the title of the Earl of Crampton."

Miss Gregory's breath caught, and Robert smiled sadly at her obvious surprise.

"It was so unexpected. I shall not go into the complexities of the matter but needless to say, one moment I was a merchant's son and the next, an Earl. Uncertain and unsure, I attempted to do all I could to gain the manner of an Earl, and only when I felt myself a little improved did I dare to make my way to London."

"And that was last Season?"

He nodded.

"It was. From the very first day I set foot in town, I

found myself fighting doubt and uncertainty. I was sure that I did not belong in amongst the *ton* and my greatest fear was that whispers and rumors would be spread all around London about me. I was not sure how I should make a respectable match when the time came, if I was considered the most ridiculous of fellows. And thus, when the situation with Lady Charlotte came about, I clung to all that the Duke of Strathaven offered me and used it to ensure my good standing in society. And since then, I have held fast to that one moment so that I do not lose myself in doubts and fear any longer."

"That is... very intriguing, Lord Crampton."

His mouth hitched into a half-smile.

"It has taken a great deal of inward determination to even speak to you of my past, Miss Gregory. It is not that I am ashamed of it but rather that I fear I will be shamed because of it." His lips pinched but his heart softened, as though relieved he was finally able to speak openly to another. "You are right that I have been arrogant and filled with pride, and I recognize that I have sought those two aspects of my character out so that I will not give way to my own deeply hidden fears. I sought the assurance and the accolades of others in the *ton* as a silent promise that they would not speak ill of me. I made certain to show myself in as good a light as possible so that no one would even *think* to enquire into my past situation – for those of the *ton* look down on those who engage in commerce. I have behaved poorly, Miss Gregory, and it is only thanks to your blunt frankness and that of Lord Venables that I have come to see myself so. As I have said, I am grateful for your opinion and shall make endeavors not to behave so any longer, if it will be an improvement to my character." A gentle smile lingered on his lips as he turned to look at her, seeing the astonishment in her wide eyes. "You speak very well and without restraint, although you are kind in your manner. I do appreciate that."

The lady blinked quickly, seeming surprised, only to then smile back at him with just the very hint of a blush in her cheeks.

"That is kind of you to say. I – I am a little honored that you have spoken to me with such honesty."

"It is the very least of what you deserve, although I pray that you would not think that any explanation is to be used as an excuse. It is certainly not my intention."

Her hand squeezed his arm lightly and Robert's heart lifted.

"I certainly do not think so."

He took in a great gulp of air, feeling as though a tight band had loosened from his chest.

"Forgive me for changing the subject so abruptly but I must ask," he continued, "what was the reason that you knocked the glass from my hand? How did you know that there was something in it?"

Miss Gregory's eyes widened and, for just a few moments, she stopped walking altogether, staring up at him with evident horror.

"Oh, but of course!" she breathed, as Robert looked back at her carefully, not certain as to why she seemed so surprised. "You could not know *why* I did such a thing!"

"No," he replied, truthfully, "I do not – although I am grateful for it."

She closed her eyes, then laughed a little ruefully.

"I did not think of that," she said softly, as they began to walk together again. "I saw a footman."

He frowned.

"A footman? There were many, were there not?"

"Yes, of course, but this one was standing to one side of the room, holding a tray with a single glass resting upon it. He did not appear at all deferential, for he was gazing across the room, looking at each and every person as though he were the master of the house and wanted to see how his guests were enjoying the evening!"

"That is a little strange, certainly," Robert agreed, his brows pulling together. "And then this footman was the one who came to me with said glass?"

"Precisely," came the reply. "And I felt nothing but alarm and thus, attempted to pull the glass from your hand but, in doing so, splashed it everywhere and greatly upset you in the process!"

Robert shook his head, his free hand reaching across to pat Miss Gregory's hand as it rested on his other arm.

"You do not know how grateful I am, Miss Gregory," he replied, fervently. "Despite what I said, despite my first, poor reaction, I am truly grateful for all that you have done." Warmth began to spread up his arm from where his fingers met hers and Robert quickly pulled his hand away, suddenly unable to look down into her eyes. Clearing his throat so that he would no longer feel such a strange awkwardness, Robert tried to smile, tried to make light of what he had said. "I do not think I would be alive had you not done so!" He had meant the sentence to be lightly jesting but the gasp from Miss Gregory's lips said otherwise. Robert winced inwardly, opening his mouth to say something more by way of explanation, only for Miss Gregory to shake her head.

"You were *very* ill, I know," she said, quietly, her cheeks now a little pale as she recalled what had taken place. "Do you think you might have....?"

She did not finish the sentence, but Robert knew what she meant, giving her a small, wry smile.

"It may have been a good deal worse, certainly," he replied, honestly. "That is the second time you have been of such great assistance to me, Miss Gregory. I should keep you close for fear that I will succumb the next time!"

"You fear there will be a next time?"

Robert hesitated, turning to her, and looking down into her eyes.

"I do not know what to think," he said, softly. "I believe that someone is attempting to injure me severely, yes. I do not know who it is nor why they are doing so." A tight hand squeezed his heart, a swirl of nervousness in his stomach. "But I shall have to find them out."

"I will help you where I can."

Again, a pink had come into her cheeks but the fervency in her eyes was unmistakable. Robert felt a surge of relief combined with gratitude bubble up within him, chasing away his nervousness. He did not deserve this kindness from her, not after how he had treated her.

"You are much too kind, Miss Gregory," he said, seeing her eyes fixed to his, clearly eager to hear what his response would be. "I do not think that I deserve such compassion from you. Nor do I understand why you would be so eager to assist me."

The color in her cheeks heightened but she did not look away.

"I mayhap cannot explain it fully myself, Lord Crampton," she said, "but that does not mean that I will not offer my assistance, albeit as little as it is. As a companion, I was able to stand and watch, and see the footman, but I am not able to converse and engage with those near to me." She tried to smile but it was a little dimmed. "If in my present situation, I can do anything to be of aid to you, then I shall do it without hesitation. I did not like seeing you so unwell and, given that the fall from the carriage could have had greater consequence had we not found you when we did, I cannot simply stand by and allow you to face this danger yourself."

"Then I shall accept your kindness, of course, but I do not think that I deserve even the sweetness of your company, Miss Gregory," he replied, truthfully. "You are much too delightful for someone such as I." The weight of his mistakes lay heavy upon his shoulders, and it took some moments for him to release himself from it. Taking a deep breath, he gave her a small smile. "The problem presented to us, however, is that I have very little understanding or knowledge of where we ought to begin."

Miss Gregory nodded slowly, turning her head away from him as she thought. Some moments of silence passed as they walked together, the only sound that of their feet on the path – and then Miss Gregory looked up at him and smiled.

"Then mayhap I should be brave," she said, as Robert frowned in confusion. "Lady Albina has been encouraging me to ask my aunt for an opportunity to be by her side as her niece, rather than her companion."

Robert's heart slammed hard against his chest without any real explanation as to why it had done so, just as a broad smile settled on his lips.

"If I am permitted to do so, then I would be able to speak with some of the young ladies who I know were present on the evening of the soiree," she continued, speaking a little more quickly now. "As a companion, I am not permitted to be introduced to them nor converse with them, but as a young lady in her own right, I..."

"You would have every opportunity to do so," he interrupted, as Miss Gregory nodded. "Miss Gregory, I think that an excellent suggestion – not because it would benefit me but because I truly believe that it is right for you to be a young lady of society rather than your aunt's companion." He tilted his head. "Might I ask if there is a reason that your aunt has not done such a thing already? Why has she never considered that idea?"

A flash of pain crossed Miss Gregory's face as she turned her head away.

"To be frank, Lord Crampton, it is because she is only inclined to think of herself and her own situation. *She* wants to marry again so that her situation, in her later years, is a little improved from the circumstances she has at present."

"That is most selfish."

A tiny, flickering smile pulled at Miss Gregory's mouth and Robert instantly felt a flush of shame, knowing all too well that he was of the very same character. He had thought only of himself, of the attention *he* would garner, of the delights which *he* would find in the company of others. To her credit, Miss Gregory did not say a word about the similarities between himself and her aunt but simply continued explaining her situation without remark.

"If I could convince her to give me one evening, one opportunity to prove that I can find gentlemen to dance and converse with me, then she might be willing to remove me as a companion and instead look at me solely as her niece."

The fervency which rose within him could not be held back. Robert stopped walking and threw a glance over his shoulder, seeing that Lady Langdon was distracted by an acquaintance. Turning back towards Miss Gregory, he took both of her hands in his, looking down into her eyes and seeing the way that she looked back at him steadily – not afraid or overcome, but calm, ready to listen to whatever it was he wanted to say.

"I will dance with you, Miss Gregory," he promised. "I will seek you out and give you two dances, even if that makes people whisper a little. I will introduce you to others – Lord Venables, for example, would be glad to stand up with you. Speak to your aunt. Beg her for the opportunity and I can promise you that you will not be disappointed." There came a small, uncertain smile which, after a few moments, grew steadily until Robert could practically see the hope growing in her eyes. Her hands pressed his and Robert finally, reluctantly, released them – all too aware that Lady Langdon was soon to end her conversation and might see them in such a stance. "I say this not for my benefit, Miss Gregory," Robert finished, his brow furrowing as he realized that she might have mistaken his fervency for this action to be solely for his advantage. "I think this would be best for *you*. Even if you do not manage to find out anything in particular as regards my difficulties, I do not care. I..."

He trailed off, realizing with a shock that, for the first time in a long time, he was not thinking at all about himself. Blinking rapidly, he dropped his head and let out a long breath, a little overcome.

"I will speak to my aunt."

His head rose and as he looked into Miss Gregory's shining eyes, his heart suddenly lifted with the joy that now filled him, glad that she would no longer have to be only a companion – even if that were only for a short while.

Would you consider her?

The question burned into his mind, but Robert did not allow himself to either contemplate or answer it. There was too much joy at this moment, too much hope and expectation, and Robert wanted Miss Gregory to feel every single second of it.

"I am so glad," he said, softly. "Pray do inform me the moment that you have her answer, Miss Gregory." He smiled at her, seeing the slight color in her cheeks. "I will be waiting."

CHAPTER TEN

"Aunt?"

The pounding of Honora's heart was so loud she was afraid her aunt would hear it.

"Yes, Nora?"

Her aunt looked back at her lazily, resting now in an armchair with a tea tray in front of her. Honora had not been invited to join her but this, Honora hoped, had not been out of a genuine disinterest in having her niece present but more due to the fact that her aunt was a single-minded, selfish creature who would not even have thought about what Honora herself might enjoy.

"I have something to ask you."

"Indeed?" Lady Langdon put a small, somewhat superficial smile on her face and beckoned Honora closer. "If you are to ask me about Lord Norrington, then I am afraid I cannot answer you as yet! He is a most amiable gentleman and has taken tea twice with me this last week!"

"Yes, aunt, I recall," Honora replied, having been present for both occasions but left to sit quietly in the corner of the room without having even been introduced to the gentleman. It appeared that he was certainly interested in her aunt's company, but whether or not anything would be forthcoming of a more permanent nature, Honora and her aunt were yet to see. "It is not about Lord Norrington, aunt. It is about my situation."

This made Lady Langdon's smile shatter in an instant, her brow furrowing.

"Your situation?"

"I am your companion and have been grateful to you for my time in London thus far," Honora said, her words tumbling out over each other in an effort to have them all spoken before she lost her nerve. Her stomach was swirling, her back stiff, and her hands clenching into fists over and over again as she held them behind her back. "But I should like to be given the opportunity to see if I can find a match."

Lady Langdon blinked in surprise and then, much to Honora's horror, laughed aloud.

"My dear girl, there is no possible way that you would *ever* be able to find a match!" she exclaimed, as though Honora had said the most mirthful thing that she had ever had the opportunity to hear. "Your father is almost destitute! You have no dowry and no gentleman in all of England would want a connection such as that!"

The words stung and Honora winced, all too aware of tears threatening – only for Lord Crampton to come to mind. She recalled how he had looked at her, the eagerness in his voice and the hope building in his eyes... and Honora felt her strength return.

"You may believe that to be true, aunt, and I will not pretend that it is at all likely that I will be able to achieve a match, but I would still like the opportunity to try."

Her aunt shook her head.

"It is a foolish endeavor."

"But one which I should like to take on regardless," Honora insisted, moving a little closer. "For example, there is a ball tomorrow evening. Could I not go as your niece rather than your companion? And," she continued, warming now to her subject as her nerves began to disappear, "if I receive no offers to dance, no interest from any gentleman, then I will, of course, return to being your companion without a word of complaint and shall never mention such a thing again."

This seemed to spark an interest in Lady Langdon for, whilst she still frowned, she did not immediately refuse Honora's request. Instead, she tipped her head, considering. Honora bit her lip, refusing to say another word until her aunt had made her decision, silently praying that she would be granted this one, single opportunity.

"A wager then, Honora," her aunt said, rising from her chair and coming towards Honora, her hand reaching out to tip up Honora's chin just a little. "One evening. One ball. If you manage to dance with at least three gentlemen, then I will consider no longer keeping you as my companion and will make certain you are introduced to the monarch and have your full introduction to society. However," she continued, a gleam in her eye which told Honora she was certain of winning this particular wager, "if you do not manage to achieve this, then you will return to being my companion and you will never again think that such a thing is possible. You will not search for another opportunity, will not demand anything of me and, in turn, will stop speaking to any gentleman or lady in that forthright manner which I find so very disagreeable."

Honora nodded, putting her trust in Lord Crampton's words, and praying that he would do just as he had promised. Then her aunt spoke again.

"And if you lose, you will not engage with Lord Crampton again. Ever. Not a single word."

A ragged breath was pulled into Honora's chest as she looked into her aunt's eyes and saw the determination there. The thought of being unable to converse with Lord Crampton again was a distressing one and Honora struggled to even think about what such a situation would be like.

But she could not let her fear and anxiety take this opportunity from her. Lord Crampton had assured her that he would dance with her and that he would introduce her to others who would be glad to stand up with her also. Taking in a deep breath, Honora nodded her consent, trusting that the scenario her aunt had set out as a consequence would never come to pass.

"Very well, aunt," she said, seeing the slight smile on her aunt's face as Lady Langdon turned away. "You have your wager. Three dances and I will gain the chance to be treated as an equal rather than a companion."

"We shall see if you will succeed," her aunt replied in a sing-song voice, letting Honora know that she thought her bound to fail. "And mayhap this will teach you, Honora, to be grateful for what you have *and* what you have been given."

Honora closed her eyes, swaying gently on the spot as she took in what this now meant. She would not have to hide in the shadows, would not have to stand as a mute, downcast young lady as her aunt regaled her acquaintances with sparkling conversation. She would no longer have to watch the dancers with eager yet sorrowful eyes, knowing now that *she* had the opportunity to stand up with them, to be counted as one of them – and to have a gentleman dance with her, just as the other young ladies did.

Lord Crampton.

A flicker of a smile pulled at Honora's lips as she hurried from the room, leaving her aunt in solitude once more. There was a growing excitement now deep within her heart. She was going to be able to dance – and to dance with none other than Lord Crampton, a gentleman whom she had thought so little of and yet now found herself looking forward to being not only in his company, but in his arms.

I will be waiting.

Honora's cheeks warmed as she hurried to the drawing-room, ready to write to him just as he had asked.

"I am able to dance with you, Lord Crampton," she murmured aloud, as though he could hear her. "And I am looking forward to that moment already."

~

"AND A VERY GOOD evening to you, Miss Gregory."

Honora dropped into a curtsey, praying silently that it was without fault. The Duke and Duchess of Strathaven were standing nearby and, whilst Honora was meant to be concentrating on greeting their host, she could not help but find herself being a little distracted by their presence.

"I am sure that this evening will be a delightful one," Lady Hoskins said, as Honora smiled at her, pulling her eyes away from the Duke. "I have heard that your aunt is to give you this evening to behave as any other young lady might, Miss Gregory."

"That is true, Lady Hoskins, and very kind of my aunt also," Honora replied, as her aunt smiled and nodded beside her. "I am sure to enjoy this evening. I thank you for your kind invitation. It will be a most exceptional ball, I am sure."

"And now I will thank *you* for your kind words," Lord Hoskins replied, as his wife smiled warmly back at Honora. "Do remember to collect your dance card from the footman before you go in. I am certain it will be full in a few moments! Go, enjoy yourself, my dear girl. And you too, Lady Langdon – although I am sure you will spend most of the evening chasing away ardent young gentlemen from your niece's company!"

"We shall see," Lady Langdon replied, only for Lord Hoskins to chuckle and Honora to blush, albeit whilst appreciating the compliment. Together, she and her aunt quickly made their way into the ballroom – leaving the Duke and Duchess of Strathaven behind.

"The *ton* is aware of this evening being of importance to you" her aunt murmured, catching hold of Honora's arm. "But whilst they may be aware of it, do *not* expect ardent gentlemen to approach you, as Lord Hoskins suggested. That idea is naught but foolishness."

"Yes, aunt," Honora replied, giving no credence to her aunt's words but allowing herself to be filled with hope – hope that Lord Crampton would soon appear.

"And Lady Charlotte is to be present – just so long as she is not hindered by another unfortunate malady."

Honora frowned. Lady Charlotte had *not* been present at the previous soiree, for it seemed that she had been taken ill – on the way to the house, in fact - and had returned home to lie down with a cold compress on her forehead. Lady Albina had told Honora that the Duchess had appeared not to be particularly concerned and Honora had been surprised at this until she learned that Lady Charlotte often had headaches and often had to stay away from social events. It was clear that the Duchess both knew, understood, and tolerated her daughter's headaches, but Lady

Albina had wondered aloud if the headaches were, sometimes, used as an excuse.

"I do not think it would improve my evening to be introduced to Lady Charlotte, aunt," she said slowly, not at all inclined to waste her time upon such things when she might otherwise be able to speak with those Lord Crampton intended to introduce her to. Besides, if Honora was honest with herself, she was not at all eager to meet the lady whom Lord Crampton had spoken of so very often. That was a little irrational, she knew, but the feeling remained regardless.

"Good evening, Lady Langdon, Miss Gregory." Lord Crampton suddenly appeared at Honora's elbow and, much to her astonishment, Honora felt her breath hitch and a fire began to ignite in her stomach. This was the most unexpected of emotions and Honora wanted to chase it away immediately but found that, for whatever reason, it chose to linger.

"Good evening, Lord Crampton," she said, as her aunt's smile faded, and ice came into her eyes.

"Good evening," Lady Langdon murmured. "Have you been enjoying the evening thus far?"

"Yes, indeed. It will be a very fine evening, I think," Lord Crampton murmured, looking into Honora's eyes as a smile pulled at his lips. "All the more improved by the company."

"You are very kind," Honora replied, aware of his compliment and finding her excitement building as she looked up at him, seeing the knowing look in his eyes. She did not have to wait for long for him to speak again.

"Now, Miss Gregory, might I be hopeful that you have not yet had your dance card filled?"

She laughed in delight, a great swell of emotion rising in

her heart as she slipped it from her hand and ignored the flash which came into her aunt's eyes.

"I have only just arrived, Lord Crampton," she told him, plainly, "and you are the first gentleman who has approached me."

"Then I shall count myself very lucky indeed," he replied, smiling as he took it from her. "Thank you, Miss Gregory. I –"

"Lord Crampton."

Honora started, having not expected someone to break into their conversation in such a rude fashion. Even Lady Langdon's eyes flared in surprise as they turned to see a young lady, tall and willowy, standing by Honora's elbow.

"I wanted to come and greet you immediately since I have not yet had the opportunity."

"How very good of you, Lady Charlotte."

Lord Crampton's voice cracked, and he was surprised to see the lady who, Honora noticed, was paying neither her nor her aunt any attention whatsoever. Her lips twisted, a line forming between her brows. This young lady, even though she was the daughter of a Duke, was being very rude indeed. She ought not to have interrupted their conversation in such a way, and certainly now should be apologizing for doing so and begging to be introduced quickly, so that they would not remain strangers. Instead, it seemed, she was paying sole attention to Lord Crampton and he, in turn, was staring back at the lady with wide eyes, clearly having forgotten entirely about Honora's dance card.

A stone dropped into her stomach.

"I had heard that you had taken unwell at the last soiree you attended, Lord Crampton." Lady Charlotte's eyes softened in concern and, much to Honora's frustration, she moved slightly so that Lord Crampton was forced to turn to keep in conversation with her. In doing so, however, he was pulled away from Honora and her aunt, leaving Honora to become a little anxious, now afraid that he would forget what he had been about to do.

"I am recovered, I thank you," Honora heard Lord Crampton say, only for Lady Charlotte to move again, pulling Lord Crampton even further away from them. "I was sorry not to be able to introduce myself to your father and mother again, of course."

"Of course." Lady Charlotte smiled and then gestured to her left. "I should be glad to take you to them now, if you wish?" she asked, making Honora catch her breath. "They are just over here."

Honora knew before Lord Crampton had even taken a step, that he would go with Lady Charlotte. Despite all that she had discussed with him, despite all that they had shared, the Duke and Duchess of Strathaven still held such a great amount of importance in Lord Crampton's mind that he would not deny himself the chance to reacquaint himself with them. Her shoulders dropped as he moved away without hesitation, clearly unaware that he still held her dance card. Closing her eyes, Honora wondered at the stab of pain which thrust itself into her heart, not certain why it was there and yet feeling its sting nonetheless.

"He still has your dance card, Honora!" Lady Langdon exclaimed, as Honora nodded, turning her head away so that she would not have to watch Lord Crampton retreating still further away from them. "That will not do at all!"

"I shall obtain another, aunt," Honora replied, her voice thin and her throat tight as hot tears began to form in the corners of her eyes. Given that she had only just stepped into the ballroom and the footman who had held the tray with the dance cards would still be present. "I will not be a moment."

She left before her aunt could either protest or prevent her. There was something of a struggle deep within her heart and Honora required a few quiet moments in which to resolve it. Making her way slowly to the door where the footman stood, Honora dropped her head and took in a deep breath, all too aware of the pain which still seared her heart.

Lord Crampton had disappointed her, had let her down when he had promised that he would not. Her dance card was held in his hand, still empty, still without a single name upon it.

And somehow, she had to find three gentlemen willing to dance with her, else all would be lost.

Dragging in a ragged breath, Honora lifted her chin and steeled herself. She could do this without Lord Crampton, she told herself sternly. She could achieve her goal of three gentlemen to dance with her. She could find Lady Albina and beg for her help – provided she had been invited to this particular ball. Turning to the footman, she held out one hand.

"I require another," she told the man, who quickly obliged her. Slipping the ribbon over her wrist, Honora turned back to make her way to her aunt, only to spy Lord Crampton bowing towards the Duke of Strathaven. She stopped, suddenly unable to remove her eyes from him. Lady Charlotte was to his left, her eyes fixed to the man whilst Lord Crampton, it seemed, was now taken up in conversation with the Duke himself. Honora's heart let out a pained cry, but she did not let it express itself on her features. Lady Charlotte was already acquainted with Lord Crampton and, given that she owed him a great debt, it was quite right that she should fawn over him so. Tightening her jaw, Honora made to turn away, made to force her eyes away from him, only to see him glance down at his hand and to then realize that he still held her dance card.

Her heart stopped. Would he acknowledge it? Would he be aware of what he had done, and make an effort to depart from the Duke to approach her again? She did not have to wait for long. Lord Crampton turned the card over in his hand, lifted his head, smiled at Lady Charlotte, and then slipped the card into his pocket.

Honora dropped her head.

Foolishness, she told herself sternly, trying to fight against the pain which forced itself through her frame with a renewed determination. *Why must you be so foolish? Lord Crampton means nothing to you other than an acquaintance! Not long ago, you thought him the most dislikeable gentleman in all of England! You were unwise to trust him and utterly idiotic to allow your heart to be so softened.*

"But I still do not think him so dislikeable now," she admitted to herself softly, lifting her head and taking a moment so that the heat in her cheeks would dissipate a little. "He *is* changed."

It was a small change, certainly, but there was so much potential that he would change still further. After all, he had been willing to listen to what she had to say and had not shot out a harsh rebuttal. In fact, he had been the one who had *asked* to hear what she had to say – and Honora knew she had not held back the truth. Biting her lip, she shook her head and, taking in a deep breath, began to walk forward as she attempted to compose herself. There was a little jealousy there and Honora reprimanded herself for feeling such a thing. To be envious of Lady Charlotte's attention to Lord Crampton, as well as seeing how he responded to her, was nothing but foolishness. There was only a small friendship – if she could call it that - between herself and Lord Crampton which meant, therefore, she had no reason to feel any sort of jealousy.

"Ah, there you are, my dear."

Honora looked at her aunt in surprise, a little taken aback by the sympathy in her voice and the gentle way she referred to her.

"I am sorry if I was a little tardy."

"I do hope you are not too discomposed?"

"Discomposed?" Honora repeated, forcing a smile that she did not really feel. "I am quite all right, aunt."

"Lord Crampton was *very* rude," her aunt replied, shaking her head, and then sending a hard look towards Lord Crampton's back, as though he would be able to feel it. "Lady Charlotte was also most improper. She may well be the daughter of a Duke and I understand that most gentlemen would be distracted by such a lady, but that does not mean that she ought to have behaved so."

Honora gave her a sad smile, whilst still being a little astonished at her aunt's upset on her behalf.

"I agree, aunt," she murmured, unable to help a glance over her shoulder towards Lord Crampton. Why was it that *he* was the only one she wanted to dance with, when so many other gentlemen were present? Why did her heart still pain her so? Frustrated with her own swirling emotions, Honora lifted her chin and set her shoulders. She was *not* going to spend the entire evening thinking about Lord Crampton. No, she would enjoy herself regardless and prove to herself that she did not need Lord Crampton's help to achieve her one and only aim for this evening.

"Miss Gregory?"

Looking into the face of a gentleman she did not immediately recognize, Honora tried to smile, throwing back all thought of Lord Crampton.

"Yes?"

"Lord Venables," he said, putting one hand to his heart. "Forgive me, I know we have not been properly introduced, but given all that Lord Crampton has said of you, I feel as though we are acquainted already!"

Warmth washed through Honora for a moment, wondering just what it was that Lord Crampton had said of her, certain that not all of it would be positive.

"He thinks very highly of you, Miss Gregory," Lord Venables continued, as though he knew exactly what she was thinking. "I think that you have come to mean a great deal to him – and that, unfortunately, has set him off balance!" He chuckled, then shook his head. "I am afraid I have spoken with too much openness, Miss Gregory. Forgive me. I came to greet you in the hope that I might ask you for a dance this evening. I have heard that you are not to be considered your aunt's companion for this ball and, thus, thought it best to make sure I had the opportunity to step out with you."

Honora's throat constricted and for some moments, she was not able to either move or speak. The relief that poured through her was all-encompassing, making her sway for just a moment as she dropped her gaze to her new dance card, managing to slip it from her wrist with trembling fingers.

I will be able to succeed this evening, she told herself, as Lord Venables thanked her. *Lord Crampton may not have done as he promised, but I will not fail. I cannot fail.*

"I am certain the entire room will be watching as I lead you out to dance, Miss Gregory," Lord Venables murmured, as he looked over the dances on the card. "You will be a hidden beauty finally revealed and I shall have the great honor of being the gentleman to dance with you."

Honora expected to feel the same heat in her cheeks which came when Lord Crampton had complimented her, but it did not instantly appear. Oddly, as she watched Lord Venables take not one but two dances, Honora realized that, aside from relief, she felt no anticipation, no excitement, and not even the smallest flicker of delight. As she accepted back her dance card Honora realized that she might, unfortunately, have to consider the fact that Lord Crampton was becoming dearer to her than she had ever expected.

And that thought frightened her more than she could say.

CHAPTER ELEVEN

"How very good to see you again, Lord Crampton."

Robert, who had been feeling a mixture of both nervousness and excitement ever since Lady Charlotte had appeared beside him, bowed quickly and then turned to bow towards the Duchess also.

"Good evening, Your Grace," he replied, repeating himself as he greeted the Duchess. "I am delighted to be in company with you again."

"Of course." The Duke of Strathaven smiled indulgently, as though he had expected nothing less from Robert. "We were sorry that you were taken ill previously, else we would have come to speak with you then."

"A small upset," Robert replied quickly, glancing down at whatever it was he held in his hand, before folding it up quickly and placing it in his pocket. "Lady Charlotte was just saying the same." Turning to face the lady in question, he smiled and inclined his head just a little. "I am grateful for your concern, but I am much recovered now."

The Duchess gestured to her daughter.

"Lady Charlotte has been looking forward to seeing you again, Lord Crampton, so that she might express the depths of her gratitude for your assistance last Season," she said, as Lady Charlotte dropped her gaze to the floor demurely. "It was so much of a shock and ordeal that it took my daughter some time away from London before she was able to recover her senses fully again."

"I quite understand, and I had no expectation of thanks being given," Robert replied, hurriedly, not wanting Lady Charlotte to be at all obliged. "I must hope that you have a much improved Season this year, Lady Charlotte. I am certain that every gentleman in London will be eager for your company." Hesitating, he took in a long breath and then forced a smile, speaking quickly due to his sudden nervousness. "In fact, Lady Charlotte, are you to dance this evening? I should very much like to ask for your dance card if that is your intention."

But what of Miss Gregory?

The quiet voice of his conscience suddenly had Robert stopped dead, his hand outstretched towards Lady Charlotte and a coldness going over his frame which had him shivering for a moment. What had he done? He had been talking to Miss Gregory and her aunt and, the very next moment, had found himself conversing with the Duke and Duchess of Strathaven and their daughter! Had he truly just left her standing there, watching him depart with Lady Charlotte? It had not been a conscious departing, but that in itself was a very great mistake! Was not this evening of the very greatest importance? Why had he allowed himself to become so distracted by promise of being reintroduced to the Duke of Strathaven that he had forgotten all about what he had promised to her?

"Lord Crampton?"

Blinking, Robert looked down to see Lady Charlotte attempting to place her dance card in his hand, but that he was not accepting it from her.

"Oh, of-of course," he stammered, feeling utterly ridiculous. "Thank you, Lady Charlotte."

His vision seemed to blur as he looked down at the dance card, finding the words difficult to make out as his chest rose and fell with quickened breaths. More than anything, he wanted to step away, to go in search of Miss Gregory and to give her the apology he knew that she deserved – but of course, he could not. Not when he was in company with such an esteemed family as this. They would take such a departure very badly indeed and would think most ill of him. Suddenly, the thought of dancing with Lady Charlotte seemed to be incredibly sour, his eagerness to be in company with the Duke again sending burning guilt and mortification through his heart.

"The polka?" he asked, handing back Lady Charlotte's card. "I have not danced that in some time, but I do very much enjoy it."

Lady Charlotte frowned.

"I am surprised that you have only taken one dance, Lord Crampton," she said, suggesting to him by her words that she would have been contented with him taking more. "And the polka, indeed!" Her gaze softened and she lifted one eyebrow enquiringly. "I would have thought you might have wished for the waltz."

Again, there came the suggestion to Robert that Lady Charlotte was not only eager for his company but that she also sought a closer acquaintance with him than they shared at present. Robert, having wondered in the past if such a thing might ever take place, did not find himself at all delighted or pleased. In fact, he found himself a little embarrassed to have her speaking in such a forward manner and simply expecting him to acquiesce. The fact that she still held her dance card in her hand rather than slipping it back onto her wrist, as well as the expectant look in her eye, made it clear to Robert that she now expected him to ask for the dance card back again so that he might add his name to the waltz as well as dancing the polka.

The problem was that Robert did not wish to. He wanted nothing more than to find Miss Gregory and to beg for her to give him another opportunity. If he could, he would take the waltz and, as he tried to smile back at Lady Charlotte, Robert found his desire to dance with Miss Gregory far exceeded anything else.

"Alas, I am already promised for the waltz," he lied, finding no other excuse to make other than that for fear that, if he was truthful, he would bring down the wrath of the Duke onto his head. "Another time, however, I should be more than glad to dance the waltz with you, Lady Charlotte. Forgive me for being unable to do so at present."

The girl's face fell. Clearly, she had been eager to dance with him, and whilst Robert did not want to disappoint her, neither did he wish to give her the wrong impression.

"But of course, Lord Crampton, we quite understand," the Duchess put in, taking away from the tension which was beginning to build between Robert and Lady Charlotte. "And tell me, who is it that you are to dance with?"

The lie came easily enough to Robert's lips.

"With Miss Gregory, whom I was speaking with only a few minutes ago," he said, as Lady Charlotte eventually slipped her ribbon back over her wrist.

"Oh?" Lady Charlotte frowned, her eyes a little narrowed. "Is she not a companion to Lady Langdon?"

"She is no longer to be considered in that role," Robert

told her, quickly. "Indeed, I must beg your forgiveness and step away for a few moments as I have just discovered her dance card in my pocket and ought to return it to her straight away, for there will be other gentlemen who will wish to dance with her, I am sure."

The Duke nodded.

"But of course," he said, understandingly. "I am glad to have seen you again, Lord Crampton. I do hope you enjoy the rest of the evening."

"I thank you, Your Grace," Robert replied, glad and relieved when he was able to step away from the conversation, turning back towards where Miss Gregory and her aunt had stood.

They were not there.

A hand clasped tightly about his heart as he stepped away from the Duke, the Duchess, and their daughter, frightened now that he would not see the lady and would not be able to make amends. He had not meant to behave so poorly, and yet knew that he must have caused her a great upset and insult in leaving her as he had done. And to have taken her dance card with him at that! Robert dropped his head, heat pouring into his face as shame burned through him. He had *not* done well – and this was after he had told her only a short while ago that he did not intend to continue with such selfishness and single-mindedness!

"You do not look as delighted as I would have thought."

Robert turned his head, his attention caught by another.

"Lord Venables," he muttered, as his friend arched an eyebrow. "Good evening."

"You have just been speaking to Lady Charlotte after you have been reintroduced to the Duke and Duchess of Strathaven!" his friend exclaimed, a broad grin on his face which Robert did not return. "Why do you appear so displeased?" His smile flickered. "Did you not receive the praise you had been expecting from the Duke?"

"No, that is not my reason for displeasure," Robert shot back quickly, feeling a sense of embarrassment mingled with shame beginning to flood him. Was that truly how his friend saw him still? Was that what he expected from him? "You may very well be surprised, but I am disappointed with my own behavior."

"Oh." Lord Venables fell into step beside Robert as he began to make his way through the crowd once more. He did not sound surprised. "What did you do?"

Again, Robert found himself with a choice. Should he tell Lord Venables the truth or hide it from him? After all, his friend did not need to know the particulars but, if he chose to remain silent, Robert knew that it was solely due to his desire to protect himself... to protect his pride.

"I treated Miss Gregory with disdain – albeit unintentionally," he said, heavily, not able to lift his gaze to his friend. "Lady Charlotte appeared at my elbow, and I simply forgot about my conversation with Miss Gregory. I abandoned her and went to speak to the Duke and Duchess – all whilst holding her dance card in my hand. I have made her a promise that this evening, I am to make certain she has at last three dances for then..." He trailed off, shaking his head, realizing that he did not need to go into details about Miss Gregory's wager with her aunt. "I *must* find her."

Lord Venables' brows rose but he said nothing, considering what Robert had revealed. Robert too remained silent, looking out across the ballroom and, much to his relief, finally catching sight of Miss Gregory. She was dancing with another gentleman and Robert found his stomach dropping to the floor.

I should be dancing with her.

"I am surprised to hear you say such a thing, but I will not pretend that it is not refreshing," Lord Venables told him, as Robert shot him a quick glance. "I do not think I have ever heard you say anything critical about yourself before."

"My skills in self-reflection are sorely lacking," Robert muttered, as Lord Venables grinned a little wryly. "Both yourself, and Miss Gregory, have assisted me in improving them."

"And you seek to make amends now?" Lord Venables asked as Robert shook his head. "No?"

"I seek only to apologize," Robert replied, taking in a deep breath, and setting his shoulders as the music came to a close. "She deserves that, at the very least. Good gracious, Venables, I continually fail in my attempts to improve myself and have now injured Miss Gregory yet again." Burning coals piled on his head. "Whatever am I to do? I will have driven her away, I am certain!"

Lord Venables put one hand on Robert's shoulder, drawing his full attention. When he turned his head to look back, he saw the questioning look in his friend's eyes.

"I am to dance with Miss Gregory also, but I do not have any of the fervor nor eagerness that you exude at the present moment, Crampton," Lord Venables said, quietly. "Has she become important to you? Perhaps in a way that you do not yet want to express?"

Robert's shame increased all the more until it felt as though he were being pushed down into the floor with the weight of it all. Miss Gregory *had* become important to him and yet he had treated her as though she was nothing more than an afterthought.

"Yes," he said, a little hoarsely. "Yes, it is as you say. Which is why I am all the more ashamed of myself."

"Then tell her that," Lord Venables advised. "Look, here she comes."

Robert looked up at once. Miss Gregory was being led from the floor by Lord Guildhall, an acquaintance of both himself and Lord Venables. His gaze was fixed to her, seeing the way her eyes darted towards him and then back again, color growing in her cheeks as the gentleman glanced towards her questioningly, before turning his steps towards Robert.

As soon as Lord Guildhall and Miss Gregory stopped in front of them, he spoke.

"Miss Gregory, I shall only be a few moments," Robert said, hurriedly before the lady could protest. "I come only to express my great regret in stepping away from you without even a word of farewell. I come to apologize for taking your dance card with me on what is the most important of evenings. And I come to beg your forgiveness for my heedless and disrespectful conduct."

Miss Gregory turned her head slightly so that she would not have to look into his eyes.

"Lady Charlotte can take the attention of any gentleman, I am sure," she replied, her voice a little higher pitched than before, her words tight. "Do excuse me, Lord Crampton, I must return to Lady Langdon."

"Please, wait."

He reached out, catching her hand in his just as the gentleman began to lead her away, and Robert caught the look of frustration that crossed the lady's face. Her lips compressed a little, her jaw clenched, and her eyebrows lifted in seemingly irritated inquiry.

"Yes, Lord Crampton?" she asked, showing that same tenacity in her manner and speech which he had seen in her from the very beginning of their acquaintance. "Is there something more you wished to say?"

The challenge in her eyes caused Robert to splutter his answer, his words coming out in a rush and making his speech indistinct.

"No, Miss Gregory. I mean, that is to say that, of course, I should be glad to talk to you again and indeed, I should – that is, I *should* like to be able to talk to you again and once more express my regret over what I have done. It was not meant to injure, I assure you."

"And yet, you did cause me distress," she replied, although the sharp glint of steel slowly began to leave her gaze as she spoke, only to be replaced with a light sheen of tears which tore great, gaping holes in Robert's heart. "Thankfully, Lord Venables has been my savior. He did for me that which you had promised to do but did not. I have now three different gentlemen on my dance card and my situation, going forward, is now fixed." Her chin lifted, her eyes sparkling – but not with delight. "Whether anything shall come of it, I do not know, but my aunt can no longer call me her companion."

"I – I am to dance the waltz with you."

She closed her eyes and shook her head.

"No, Lord Crampton, you are not."

"I must," he said, taking a step closer to her as she opened her eyes to look at him. "I told Lady Charlotte that I was to do so and –" A single tear ran down Miss Gregory's cheek as she looked up at him, although she dashed it away with such force that it was as if she were embarrassed to be seen demonstrating any emotion. "Miss Gregory, I am sorry."

Robert could say nothing more, his shoulders dropping,

his head hanging low and shame filling him completely. For the first time, he saw himself as he truly was: a gentleman who thought of nothing but his situation and his own determination to remain in good standing in society. He had allowed his need to be reacquainted with the Duke of Strathaven to become most important, fearful that he would drop somewhat in the eyes of the *ton*, that they would then dredge up his past and use it to shame him. He had let it overshadow everything and everyone else.

"Miss Gregory." Broken, Robert looked up into her eyes and saw her standing very still, looking back at him with such a heaviness in her expression that he wanted to cry out in anger at the pain he had caused her. "There is nothing I can say which would further express my own sorrow and, regardless, I do not think that it would bring you any relief. I can see now, Miss Gregory, just how small a man I am." For the first time, he spoke without a single modicum of hesitation, wanting to express the truth to her, wanting her to know what she had brought out in him. "I have been concerned with myself and my own circumstances and have not given even a single thought to anyone else. You, for example, have found yourself in such a difficult circumstance that I do not know how you have borne it! And yet I was oblivious to your trouble, reminding myself that you were only a companion when, in truth, I ought to have seen you as the lady you are, ought to have thought about just how painful you must be finding your situation, from the very beginning. And then, when I promised to help you, when I gave you my word, for me only to pull away from you, to allow myself to be distracted by my own selfishness yet again... I cannot imagine how you must be feeling at this present moment, Miss Gregory. You have every right to despise me, to turn from me, and I shall not blame you if you choose to do so. However, I will tell you truthfully that I will forever be grateful for you and our connection. Your frankness and outspokenness have forced me to look at myself in a way which I strongly dislike!" He smiled sadly, aware of the gentle glistening in Miss Gregory's eyes, and finding the sorrow still rising within his own heart. "It has taken me some time, but I see now that every word you spoke to me was true. I will be a better fellow from this day forward, Miss Gregory, and it will be because of you."

Silence grew between them for some moments after Robert had stopped speaking. Miss Gregory held his gaze with unblinking emerald eyes, studying him, watching him, considering what he had said. No further tears had fallen but Robert knew that they were not too far away, feeling guilt squeeze his heart once more that *he* was the cause of it.

"I do hope, Miss Gregory, that you will step aside?"

The harsh voice of Lady Charlotte suddenly broke in, between them, and the lady came forward without hesitation, standing next to Robert and fixing a hard gaze on Miss Gregory.

"I – I beg your pardon?" Miss Gregory asked, looking at Lady Charlotte in bewilderment – the very same bewilderment which Robert himself felt.

"Lord Crampton said he could not dance the waltz with me since he was to stand up with *you*," Lady Charlotte sniffed, her gaze going up and down Miss Gregory's form as though she were assessing her. "But I do hope that he has explained the situation to you and that you will step aside?"

Robert dropped his shoulders and closed his eyes. After what he had done to Miss Gregory, he knew that she owed him nothing and would, most likely, agree that Lady Charlotte could dance with him for the waltz. He deserved no favors from her.

"I – I think not."

Miss Gregory's response hit him hard, making Robert catch his breath as he lifted his head, seeing her standing tall, her chin lifted, irresolute.

"I beg your pardon?"

Now it was Lady Charlotte's turn to sound confused and Robert, seeing the determination in Miss Gregory's face, took a small side-step towards her.

"I have not explained the circumstances to Miss Gregory, Lady Charlotte," he said so that Miss Gregory would not have to make an explanation. "I still intend to dance the waltz with her, as I had hoped."

Lady Charlotte's face went puce. Her eyes narrowed and she glared at Miss Gregory as though it were her fault that such a thing had happened. Not a word was spoken until, finally, she turned away and departed their company without further remark. Robert took another small step closer to Miss Gregory, glancing down at her and smiling softly when her gaze reached his.

"Thank you, Miss Gregory," he murmured, as she finally returned his smile. "It is a favor I do not deserve from you."

Her eyes flickered for a moment.

"Your words were honest and true," she said, softly. "I believe that you meant every word, and now, to choose me over the Duke's daughter..." Her smile grew and she lifted one shoulder in a half shrug. "I am honored."

"The honor is mine, in being able to stand up with you, Miss Gregory," he told her, humbly. "I look forward to dancing the waltz with you."

A gentle sparkle came into her eyes.

"As do I, with you," she murmured, as a happiness which Robert had never known before rose up within his heart and embraced him completely – and all because of the astonishing Miss Gregory.

CHAPTER TWELVE

"And so the wager is won."

Honora smiled at her aunt, seeing the grimace on her face, and realizing that she had truly believed that Honora would never succeed.

"It is, aunt," she replied, as calmly as she could. "I am no longer to be considered your companion but as a young lady in my own right, here for the Season and giving all of my efforts to finding a husband."

This last remark brought a scornful exclamation to her aunt's lips, but Honora did not allow it to influence her or pull away at her happiness. Last evening had been a trial but somehow, she had found a happiness through it which seemed to pervade every last fiber of her being. The way Lord Crampton had spoken to her, the fervor with which he had apologized, had burned into her heart and left her in no doubt that he had meant every word. And then, for him to have made certain that *she* was the one he waltzed with, rather than standing up with the daughter of a Duke, had told her just how much he esteemed her, just how much he valued her – and her sorrow and upset had begun to dissipate. Waltzing with him had been a dream, and Honora had every moment of it fixed in her memory. And the feelings which had filled her as she had stood up with him had not left her since.

"You will not find a husband," her aunt replied – again, not attempting to be unfeeling but intending to express the truth to Honora so that she would not feel such an uncertain hope. "You may enjoy these few weeks left of the Season but nothing more will come of it."

"I can but try, aunt," Honora replied, not allowing her aunt's words to break down her happiness. "You have been most obliging."

Her aunt snorted and muttered something under her breath – which was, no doubt, a remark about how she had never expected Honora to succeed – but Honora ignored this, rising from her chair, and making her way to the door.

"I will write to father so that he is informed," she said, swiftly. "Do excuse me."

"Oh, Honora, wait a moment."

She turned.

"Yes, aunt?"

"If you are thinking that Lord Crampton might be the one who saves you from your life of poverty, might I encourage you to remove such a thought from your mind."

Honora's stomach tightened, her bright smile fading.

"I do not understand."

"He is to be wed to Lady Charlotte – or so I have heard," her aunt continued, waving a hand as though such news were meant to be dismissed easily enough. "So you should think of another, Honora. Lord Crampton is already spoken for."

"That is not so, aunt," Honora replied, firmly. "Wherever did you hear such a thing?"

"Oh, from Lady Charlotte herself!" Lady Langdon exclaimed as Honora's eyes widened. "She told me last evening that she is soon to be betrothed to Lord Crampton! An excellent match, of course, since he saved her from that ridiculous Lord Forthside. So you should be careful, Honora, not to give him too much of your attention. The fellow is going to be wed soon."

Honora tilted her head, considering. Those words had done nothing to frighten or upset her, for she knew, given her interaction with Lady Charlotte last evening, that the lady was not to be trusted. Why had she gone to speak to Honora's aunt? Was it to make sure that Honora was pushed away from Lord Crampton so that she might have the assurance of his interest for herself? But if there *was* to be a betrothal, then Lord Crampton would not be forced into such a thing, surely? Honora knew that the gentleman was of a strong mind and that to be coerced into a betrothal was not something which he would permit. There was a strong possibility, therefore, that Lord Crampton might soon fall from grace in society's eyes, for if the lady claimed a betrothal and he denied it, then they would, of course, think that *he* was at fault.

So why was Lady Charlotte saying such things, especially when Lord Crampton had been the one to save her from Lord Forthside?

Then, as she stood there, an idea hit her with such force that Honora caught her breath, one hand wrapping around her stomach as she bent forward slightly, her eyes flaring wide and her breathing ragged. Surely, it could not be! She would never have considered such a thing and yet now that she thought of it, it made sense of everything!

"Honora?" her aunt inquired, looking at her with one lifted eyebrow. "Are you quite well?"

"I – I must go!" Honora exclaimed, turning swiftly. "I have a letter to write. Excuse me, aunt."

She did not linger to hear what her aunt then called after her, desperate to pen a note to Lord Crampton immediately. If she was right, then he could find himself in danger at any moment. Honora did not think that Lady Charlotte would let anything stop her from succeeding - and that was a frightening thought indeed.

∼

Biting her lip, Honora stepped away from Lord Stapleton, having already greeted him warmly and thanked him for his invitation. Her aunt had been less than pleased at having to introduce Honora as her niece rather than her companion, but Honora had barely heard it and certainly had not even the smallest consideration for what her aunt thought or felt. The only person on her mind was Lord Crampton. She had written her note with only a few hours to spare before this evening's event and could not tell whether or not he had received it, for there had come no reply. That might well have been due to the fact that he had been at the fashionable hour or otherwise engaged in another matter, but Honora had spent every minute doing nothing but worrying and waiting for him to reply.

And it still had not come.

"Good evening, Miss Gregory."

Honora started as Lady Albina came towards her. Her friend was smiling warmly, her eyes bright and her hands outstretched so that she might clasp Honora's hands in her own.

"I have heard that you are no longer to be introduced nor seen as a companion to your aunt!" she exclaimed, as

Honora nodded, trying to smile and focus on her friend even though her eyes were eager to continue searching the room for Lord Crampton. "My very sincere congratulations. I knew that you could be bold enough to ask your aunt for a wager!"

"I would not have done it without your encouragement," Honora replied, truthfully. "Thank you, Lady Albina." She cleared her throat and lowered her head just a fraction, speaking quietly. "I must, however, find Lord Crampton. It is of the utmost importance. Have you seen him?"

Lady Albina frowned.

"No, I have not," she replied, looking at Honora curiously. "Is there something wrong?"

Honora nodded.

"I believe so," she said, unwilling to go into a long and convoluted explanation. "I have written to him, but he did not reply. I *must* speak with him - it is very urgent."

"Then allow me to help you find him," Lady Albina said, firmly. "Come, Miss Gregory. We will do so together."

Without even a backward glance towards her aunt, Honora linked arms with Lady Albina and began to make her way through the house. Lord Stapleton had opened his drawing-room, library, parlor, and dining room for this grand soiree which, Honora knew, would soon have various entertainments throughout. The library was for card games, the dining room would have refreshments and dancing and music would take place in the drawing-room.

"He could be anywhere in this house, if he is here at all," she murmured aloud, speaking half to herself. "I *must* –"

"Miss Gregory."

Honora came to a sudden stop as Lady Charlotte

suddenly swung into her path. Her eyes were bright, her smile fixed, but there was no warmth in her expression.

"Good evening, Lady Charlotte," Honora replied, as Lady Albina also murmured a greeting. "If you will excuse us, we are just going in search of -"

"I do hope that your aunt has informed you of some particular news, Miss Gregory," Lady Charlotte interrupted as if she were entirely unaware that Honora had been speaking. "I hope you understand that whatever connection you have formed with Lord Crampton can no longer be."

Honora lifted her chin, her anger mounting.

"I hardly think that a young lady making such a decision alone holds any real significance, no matter her standing," she replied, allowing her blunt manner to spread out without hindrance. "You are aware that Lord Crampton has no knowledge of this?"

Lady Charlotte chuckled and the sound sent a cold pricking all down Honora's spine.

"He will soon become aware of it, Miss Gregory," she said, reaching out to press one hand to Honora's arm, and Honora had to physically restrain herself from recoiling. "Have no doubt about that."

The urge to find Lord Crampton only grew as Honora looked into Lady Charlotte's cold eyes and, without another word, she pulled Lady Albina forward, moving around Lady Charlotte and making her way into the hallway.

"I do not understand," Lady Albina said, her brow lined as she looked at Honora with confusion. "Lord Crampton is betrothed? And to Lady Charlotte? Is that what she was implying?"

"He is not betrothed," Honora replied, grimly. "I cannot explain everything now, Lady Albina, but I shall say that

Lady Charlotte has nothing but dark intentions for Lord Crampton."

"But why?" Lady Albina asked, her voice a little breathless. "Why would she do such a thing?"

Honora was about to answer, when the very gentleman she wanted to see exited from the library and, turning, came to a stop as he caught her gaze. A broad smile spread across his handsome face and Honora let out a long breath of relief, hurrying forward and reaching out to grasp both of his hands in hers.

"Miss Gregory!" Lord Crampton exclaimed, "I –"

"It is Lady Charlotte," Honora said, breathlessly. "It is Lady Charlotte, Lord Crampton! I am sure of it!"

She gazed fervently into his eyes but saw his brows pull together, a line forming between them. Clearly, he did not understand what she meant.

"The fall from the carriage, the poison in your drink!" she exclaimed, her hands tightening on his. "They were orchestrated by Lady Charlotte - I am *sure* of it."

Lord Crampton's eyes flared, and he immediately began to shake his head, but whether this came from a lack of agreement or utter disbelief, Honora could not say.

"She intends to announce that you are betrothed," she said, lowering her voice for fear that they would be overheard by another. "My aunt states that she was informed of it only yesterday by Lady Charlotte herself!"

"Betrothed?" Lord Crampton appeared all the more stunned. "But why should she say such a thing? She has never expressed any inclination towards me, and I certainly have not considered her as my potential future bride." His thumb brushed absently over the back of her hand, his eyes holding hers. "I had never thought of any such thing about any young lady, Miss Gregory, not until recently."

Despite the tension raging through her, Honora could not help but smile, blushing gently at his tender remark, her heart soaring to the sky as she heard the quiet hope in his voice.

"So why would she say such a thing?" Lady Albina broke in, who had come to join them and was now looking at Honora in confusion. "That would bind them together, would it not? You are suggesting that she seeks to injure Lord Crampton, so why –"

"Because I will refute it," Lord Crampton said suddenly, a paleness beginning to seep into his cheeks as he realized what Honora had been trying to tell him. "I will be surprised that there is talk of a betrothal and, upon my refusing to agree to it, Lady Charlotte can then begin to act with such sorrow and sadness that I will appear to be the cruel-hearted gentleman who refused to wed the Duke's daughter."

"I fear it will be worse than that," Honora replied, softly. "I am sure that she will give reasons for your supposed betrothal so that when you refuse to accept the engagement as it stands, she can cry foul."

Lord Crampton's eyes widened, his face a little grey.

"She could accuse me of any number of things and the *ton* would believe her," he said, hoarsely. "I will be thrown from society! I will become nothing but a byword, a faded memory, and a gentleman without any respect of his own."

"Indeed," Honora murmured, as Lady Albina continued to frown. "Lady Charlotte has a great plan in place, Lord Crampton, and she can enact it at any time. Confident of her success, she spoke to me personally, telling me that there could be no connection between us any longer since the betrothal was soon to be announced."

"But *why*?" Lady Albina put in, sounding caught

between frustration and confusion. "I do not understand why she would do so, given that Lord Crampton was the one who saved her from Lord Forthside."

Honora gave her a grim smile.

"It is because of Lord Forthside that she is doing this," she said, clearly. "Whilst the *ton* and Lord Crampton and even the Duke and Duchess of Strathaven believed that Lord Crampton had saved Lady Charlotte from Lord Forthside's clutches and dark intentions, I believe it was precisely the opposite."

Swallowing hard, Lord Crampton dropped one of Honora's hands and ran his hand over his eyes.

"You think that she was attempting to escape with Lord Forthside."

"I do," Honora replied, quickly. "It does make sense - if one thinks about it clearly. What mother would want her daughter to wed a gentleman so far below her in status? Would a Duke be content with his daughter marrying a mere Viscount?"

"No," Lady Albina agreed, softly. "No, they would not. And despite the fact that Lady Charlotte might have cared for this fellow, might have wished to wed him, her parents would not have consented."

"And thus, she tried to elope, only for me to discover them, to think that Lord Forthside was attempting to steal Lady Charlotte away against her will, and to save her from him."

"Which was not what she wanted. You inadvertently took away her happiness, her only chance of true affection between herself and her husband and, whilst she might have play-acted the part of being relieved and thankful, she has been working hard to punish you for what you did."

Lady Albina let out a long, slow breath, shaking her head gently.

"Good gracious."

"No doubt she would have been able to pay those she used to carry out her commands," Honora finished, as Lord Crampton nodded slowly, his eyes fixed to the floor and his forehead lined. "The night that you took that glass of brandy, the one which I knocked from your hand, she was not even present! No doubt she wanted nothing to do with the event itself so that she could claim to be innocent and unaware, as she was not even there that evening. Meanwhile, the footman she had, no doubt, paid to do as she asked, did what was expected, and had you not had the glass removed from you, you might well have been taken very ill indeed." A small shudder shook her frame, her hand tightening on his. "Deathly ill, mayhap."

A few moments of silence spread between them as Lord Crampton closed his eyes, pinching the bridge of his nose with his hand still holding tight to Honora's.

"I do not know what to do."

"You could confront her?" Honora asked as Lady Albina's attention was caught by a passing gentleman who began to speak to her earnestly, leaving Honora and Lord Crampton to their conversation. "Tell her that you know of what she has done and what she intends."

Lord Crampton shrugged, shaking his head.

"What good would that do?" he asked, heavily. "Even if I know all of what she has done, she can still continue with her intentions. My awareness of it does not change anything."

Honora bit her lip, suddenly feeling hopeless. Lord Crampton was right. Her knowing what Lady Charlotte intended did nothing to prevent the lady from carrying out her plan.

"I could... announce my betrothal," Lord Crampton said suddenly, his voice a little softer, a little tentative. "That would be the only way I could think of to succeed."

A swell of panic rose in Honora's chest. She dropped Lord Crampton's hand and took a step back from him, horrified that the man would consider betrothing himself to Lady Charlotte.

"But why?" she managed to say, her voice hoarse. "Why would you do such a thing?"

Lord Crampton's brows lowered into a frown.

"If I announce a betrothal, she will not be able to pretend that she is betrothed to me," he said, rendering Honora all the more confused. "That is the only solution I can see."

Honora was about to ask him what he meant and just who he would betroth himself to, when Lady Albina, who had been near enough to overhear their conversation whilst continuing with her own, turned back towards her for a moment.

"He means to betroth himself to you, Miss Gregory," she said, in a half-whisper. "To *you*. Do you understand?"

With a smile, she pressed Honora's arm and then returned to her own conversation, leaving Honora to stand, speechless, before Lord Crampton.

His face was quite red, his eyes darting from here to there without ever truly lingering on her features. He was unsure of her response, embarrassed that he had not made himself clear and now a little anxious in the lingering silence.

"You – you would wish to betroth yourself to me?"

Her voice was breathless, her hand clasped to her heart.

Lord Crampton spread his hands.

"If you would be willing," he said, slowly. "Miss Gregory, I will admit that I had not thought of matrimony during the first few weeks of our acquaintance, but I *have* begun to think of you in a way which I would never have expected." His hand was still holding hers and he took a small step closer to her, his eyes searching hers. "I had hoped that, in a few weeks, I might ask to court you, once I had proved myself to you," he continued, making Honora's eyes flare in surprise. "I know that I only recently disappointed you, that the hurt from my forgetfulness must still be painful, and I wanted to give myself time to make certain that I might, one day, become the gentleman you deserved. But now, it seems, I have no choice but to beg of you to consider me as your future husband, Miss Gregory. You are the only lady I could ever imagine as being my bride, the only lady who has ever had such an effect on my heart and mind that I cannot forget her!" A small chuckle escaped him, and Honora smiled a little bashfully. "It is, however," he continued, seriousness coming into his eyes, his smile fading, "a very great thing to ask of you. To ask you to trust me, to ask you to believe that the change in my character is a permanent one, to trust that I will provide for you, love you, and care for you as a husband ought when, only yesterday, I broke a promise to you. I understand fully if you choose not to trust me so, Miss Gregory. I will not hold it against you nor bear a grudge. In fact, I would urge you *not* to accept me, given that I still have so much to prove!"

Honora had been unable to breathe properly for the last few minutes. The astonishment of being offered a proposal of marriage was one thing, but to have it from Lord Crampton was quite another. The gentleman who had pushed her emotions from one thing to the next, the gentleman who had, as he had only just said, not yet proved himself to her, and the gentleman whom she could not seem to forget.

"I – I will accept."

Lord Crampton's eyes flared wide as Lady Albina moved tactfully away, keeping close enough to Honora to allow her a little privacy whilst being entirely within the realms of propriety.

"You know that I need to wed," Honora told Lord Crampton, seeing how the light in his eyes began to fade. "You are also aware that I have no dowry, that my father is impoverished, and should I not find a husband, I will have no future aside from that of a companion. But," she continued, taking a deep breath and allowing a wide smile to spread across her face, "those are not the reasons that I have for accepting you." The light which flooded back into Lord Crampton's eyes made Honora smile all the more. "I accept you because I believe that you *are* reforming yourself," Honora said, as Lord Crampton closed his eyes momentarily, clearly relieved. "I believe all that you said to me last evening. Your regret was real, your apology genuine. And, Lord Crampton, if I am to be truthful, I would tell you here and now that my heart has begun to fill with an affection for you which I did not ever think would be there. My mind is full of thoughts of you. When I realized about Lady Charlotte, my upset and my fright was based solely on the concern that I might lose you to her entirely!" She laughed softly as Lord Crampton caught her other hand with his, his breath dancing across her cheek, his nearness igniting deep emotion within her heart. "I accept you, Lord Crampton, because you have become more to me than I ever expected."

"I do not deserve such affection, nor kindness, nor trust," he told her, lifting her hand to his lips, and pressing a kiss to the back of her hand. "But I shall spend every day proving myself to you, Honora. I swear it to you here and now: I will be everything a husband ought to be and more. I will thank the good God above every day for the wife he has given me and will love you with all of my heart so that you never have cause to regret your choice."

The warmth of his lips on her hand spread heat all through Honora, and she blushed, dropping her gaze for a moment but unable to keep the smile from her lips.

"If you would be contented, I should like to announce it... now," Lord Crampton said, as Honora laughed. "Given my present state of happiness, I should hate it if Lady Charlotte did anything to take that away from me."

"From us both," Honora replied, slipping her arm through his and then turning back towards the drawing-room so that they might fall into step together. "Yes, let us go."

~

The butterflies which were fluttering through Honora's stomach did not desist as Lord Crampton made his announcement. Instead, they only increased, although the smile on her lips remained. Her eyes roved about the room, looking at all of the faces which were now bearing various expressions – some astonished, some smiling in delight and others barely acknowledging it at all, clearly eager to return to their conversations.

"Honora!"

The hubbub of conversation had returned as Honora heard her name being hissed, turning her head to see her aunt standing there. Lady Langdon's face was bright red, her eyes sparkling with anger.

"Whatever is the meaning of this?"

"I have proved you wrong, aunt," Honora replied, without malice. "I *have* been able to find someone willing to wed me."

Lord Crampton gave Lady Langdon a warm smile.

"I do hope that you can be glad for your niece, Lady Langdon," he said, calmly. "I can assure you that I will do all I can to make her the happiest, most contented of ladies in all of England."

"You have not gained my consent!" Lady Langdon exclaimed, as Honora stepped forward and put one hand on her aunt's arm, quietening her.

She recognized that Lady Langdon was angry with Honora's success, with the fact that Honora *had* been able to find a match when she herself had not yet done so – and when she had been proven incorrect for what was now the second time. Speaking firmly, she gazed directly into her aunt's face.

"I do not require your consent, aunt, and have every certainty that my father will give his without hesitation," she stated, firmly. "Pray attempt to find a *little* happiness in my joy, aunt. I am no longer facing the dark future of being entirely alone, and instead can now look to a day when I will belong in my own house, when I will be mistress of it and can love my husband – just as you once did." This was something which seemed to astonish Lady Langdon, for all at once, the anger left her eyes and her mouth dropped open. Honora gave her a quick smile and then stepped back, having seen Lady Charlotte just behind her aunt. "Excuse me, aunt," she murmured, before pulling Lord Crampton away.

"Lady Charlotte."

Lord Crampton's voice was low, his eyes fixed.

"This is a sham!" Lady Charlotte exclaimed, her eyes narrowing. "You have done this only so that –"

"So that you cannot force Lord Crampton to take on the punishment for something he did not deliberately do?" Honora put in, catching Lady Charlotte off guard. "You love Lord Forthside? You were to elope with him?"

In an instant, Lady Charlotte's expression crumpled. Her eyes lowered, her shoulders slumped, and Honora could see the trembling which had taken hold of her frame.

"You should feel the same pain as I," she whispered, directing her words towards Lord Crampton. "To have been so close to the only happiness I wanted, to being in the arms of the gentleman I loved..." She shook her head, her voice thick with tears. "You took that from me."

"But not deliberately," Lord Crampton put in, his voice still hard with anger. "I thought to be doing you a service, Lady Charlotte. I never even imagined that there was anything more to your connection with Lord Forthside."

Honora's heart twisted in sympathy for, whilst what Lady Charlotte had done was entirely wrong, there was great pain there and Honora could understand that.

"I could still claim that we are betrothed," Lady Charlotte sniffed, as Honora exchanged a glance with Lord Crampton. "You could still be shamed, torn apart, and broken, just as I have been."

"Or," Honora put in, one hand on Lord Crampton's arm before he could explode with fury, "you might ask for our help."

Lady Charlotte's eyes lifted to hers, confusion deep within them.

"I cannot imagine your suffering," Honora continued, gently. "But, if there is a way to assist you, a way to reunite you with Lord Forthside, then surely that is the better path to take rather than revenge?" She gave a long look towards Lord Crampton, whose brows were deeply furrowed. Giving his arm a gentle squeeze, she turned back to Lady Charlotte. "I have found a happiness and a joy which I did not expect," she finished, softly. "I cannot imagine what I would feel should it be taken from me. But Lord Crampton did not steal you from your love with any deliberate intention."

"And I will try to help you, should you wish it," she heard Lord Crampton say, allowing a small breath of relief to escape her. "All you need do is ask."

Lady Charlotte could not look at them, for she dropped her head lower still and Honora heard a small, gasping sob escape her. They stood together for some moments until, finally, Lady Charlotte lifted her head, set her shoulders, and tried to smile, despite her red-rimmed eyes.

"Mayhap you and I might begin a correspondence, Miss Gregory," she said, as Honora nodded. "I – I do not think that I deserve any such kindness but –"

"Then you are not the only one, Lady Charlotte," Lord Crampton interrupted. "Please, begin your correspondence at any time. Miss Gregory and I will be waiting."

∽

"Wonderful!"

Lord Crampton reached forward and pulled Honora into a warm embrace, spinning around the room for a moment and making her squeal with laughter. The letter from her father, giving Lord Crampton permission to marry Honora, had arrived only a few moments before.

"I knew he would consent," Honora replied, as Lord Crampton lowered her gently. She looked up into his eyes, her breath catching in her chest at the look in his eyes. "I never doubted it."

"I did," Lord Crampton confessed, a small, wry smile on his lips. "Honora, I want you to know that I have every intention of aiding your father."

Honora blinked in surprise.

"What do you mean?"

"Financially," came the reply. "I do not want him to be suffering destitution when I have more than enough! As you have told me, it is not his doing that he has fallen on such times and, if I can help him, then I shall. After all, I was once a man who knew very little of wealth and fortune. I understand the difficulties it can bring, when there is not enough - and I do not have any intention of permitting your father to endure such a situation any longer."

The lump which came into Honora's throat would not budge for some minutes, and it was all she could do to nod, her hand reaching up to brush along Lord Crampton's cheek. In the fortnight since their betrothal, Honora had learned more and more about Lord Crampton's character and had seen his continued determination to change from a prideful, selfish, arrogant gentleman into one who thought of others, who cared deeply and without reserve. And, in that time, Honora had also found her heart yearning for him all the more, having such a great and ardent affection that it could not be held back. Looking up into his gentle blue eyes, Honora found herself speaking without hesitation, her hand still resting on his cheek.

"I have come to love you, Crampton," she said, softly. "Even in this, you show such a care, such an understanding and willingness to be of aid that my heart cannot help but love you."

Lord Crampton did not answer her. Instead, he pulled

her close, his hands at her waist, her arms about his neck. When he did speak, his voice was muffled, held close to the curve of her neck.

"I do not deserve your love, Honora," he murmured. "I fear I still do not deserve *you* and yet you offer me more than I have ever dreamed of."

"As you do to me," she replied, her fingers brushing through his hair at the nape of his neck. "Somehow, despite our difficult beginning, we have found a way to love and happiness which will, I am sure, continue through the rest of our years together."

He smiled, leaned down, and brushed the lightest of kisses against her lips. "And I shall love you with all of my heart in each and every day of those years," he told her. "My precious, beautiful Honora."

I AM so glad they found their happy ever after, despite a rough beginning. I love it when Honora starts the story with nothing and it ends with her living a good life, with both prosperity and love!

PLEASE CHECK out one of my earlier books, Mistaken for a Rake Preview available ahead!

MY DEAR READER

Thank you for reading and supporting my books! I hope this story brought you some escape from the real world into the always captivating Regency world. A good story, especially one with a happy ending, just brightens your day and makes you feel good! If you enjoyed the book, would you leave a review on Amazon? Reviews are always appreciated.

Below is a complete list of all my books! Why not click and see if one of them can keep you entertained for a few hours?

The Duke's Daughters Series
The Duke's Daughters: A Sweet Regency Romance Boxset
A Rogue for a Lady
My Restless Earl
Rescued by an Earl
In the Arms of an Earl
The Reluctant Marquess (Prequel)

A Smithfield Market Regency Romance
The Smithfield Market Romances: A Sweet Regency Romance Boxset
The Rogue's Flower
Saved by the Scoundrel
Mending the Duke
The Baron's Malady

The Returned Lords of Grosvenor Square
The Returned Lords of Grosvenor Square: A Regency Romance Boxset
The Waiting Bride
The Long Return
The Duke's Saving Grace
A New Home for the Duke

The Spinsters Guild
A New Beginning
The Disgraced Bride
A Gentleman's Revenge
A Foolish Wager
A Lord Undone

Convenient Arrangements
Convenient Arrangements: A Regency Romance Collection
A Broken Betrothal
In Search of Love
Wed in Disgrace
Betrayal and Lies
A Past to Forget
Engaged to a Friend

Landon House
Landon House: A Regency Romance Boxset
Mistaken for a Rake
A Selfish Heart
A Love Unbroken
A Christmas Match
A Most Suitable Bride
An Expectation of Love

Second Chance Regency Romance
Second Chance Regency Romance Boxset
Loving the Scarred Soldier
Second Chance for Love
A Family of her Own
A Spinster No More

Soldiers and Sweethearts
To Trust a Viscount
Whispers of the Heart
Dare to Love a Marquess
Healing the Earl
A Lady's Brave Heart

Ladies on their Own: Governesses and Companions
More Than a Companion

Christmas Stories
Love and Christmas Wishes: Three Regency Romance Novellas
A Family for Christmas
Mistletoe Magic: A Regency Romance

Happy Reading!

All my love,

Rose

A SNEAK PEAK OF MISTAKEN FOR A RAKE

CHAPTER ONE

"Do hurry up, Rebecca! The carriage has been waiting for some minutes and you are, again, tardy."

Rebecca bit her lip and forced herself not to retort words she would later regret back to her father. She would have liked to have told him the reason she was a little later than he expected was that she had spent some time sorting out a strong disagreement between her twin sisters, Anna and Selina. That had been a very lengthy discussion, and thus, she had been left with very little time of her own to prepare for this afternoon's outing.

"The carriage, the carriage!" the Duke said, ushering her in. "Your sisters are waiting!"

Smoothing her skirts as she sat, Rebecca looked at her sisters enquiringly, seeing the blush on both of their faces. They knew full well that the duke had been irritated with her when the fault was entirely their own. Of course, neither of them confessed, given that their father was already irritated and they did not want to incur his wrath. A little frustrated, Rebecca turned her eyes to the window, hearing her father give instructions to the driver before he climbed into the carriage. She took a breath, letting it out slowly, dampening down her frustration.

"Now that we are *quite* ready," the Duke said, the door closed behind him, "perhaps we can finally be on our way to Madame Bernadotte." He sighed heavily. "You will have to be much more punctual from now on, Rebecca. From what I recall of London society, it is not at all acceptable to be late to soirees and dinner parties."

"Yes, Father," Rebecca replied monotonously. There was no excitement within her at the prospect of being a part of London society. Instead, there was the heavy burden of knowing that, most likely, she would have to guide her younger sisters through London in the hope that they would find suitable matches, for her father certainly would not do so. These last few years, her father had become more and more detached from his children, and Rebecca had been the one to step in where her father had failed.

Nothing would change now that they were in London, she was sure of it. He would expect her to do as she had always done. What hope did she have of finding a husband for herself when she had the responsibility of her twin sisters? It was just as well that the younger three remained at the estate in the care of their governess, else Rebecca did not know how she would have managed even to step outside the house!

"Rebecca?"

Turning her attention back to her father, Rebecca tried to smile. "Yes, Father?"

"Make sure that your sisters find what they require," he said vaguely. "I have no notion of fashion plates and the like. They will be guided by you."

Sighing inwardly and wishing that she knew what the fashion was to be this Season, she gave her father a brief nod and then returned her gaze to the window. This was going to be a very difficult Season indeed.

∼

"Oh, I beg your pardon!"

Rebecca stumbled back, heat pouring into her cheeks as she realized that she had practically walked into another lady of the *ton* without realizing it. "Are you quite all right?"

The lady laughed and put one hand out towards Rebecca. "You need not worry, my dear," she said kindly, her blue eyes sparkling. "Are you going to Madame Bernadotte's?" She gestured to the establishment just ahead of Rebecca, her smile warm and friendly.

"Yes, yes, I am," Rebecca replied, still a little embarrassed. "My father..." She closed her eyes, then opened them, taking in a deep breath. "Forgive me." Dropping into a quick curtsy, she smiled back at the older lady. "If you would permit me to introduce myself, I am Lady Rebecca. My father is the Duke of Landon. He is presently inside with my two sisters, Lady Anna and Lady Selina."

"I see," the lady replied. "Then I do not think we should keep a duke waiting, Lady Rebecca. Shall we?"

A little surprised by the lady's forwardness, Rebecca nodded and turned towards the door, all the more astonished when the lady followed after her.

"My son, it seems, has purchased me a pair of most expensive gloves," the lady continued with a wry smile. "He and I have come to London to speak to my late husband's solicitors about a few affairs. I think this gift is to encourage me to remain in London a little longer!"

Rebecca turned her head, lowering her voice as they walked inside. "I am sorry to hear of your husband's passing."

The lady smiled sadly, her expression now a little morose. "It was some years ago, Lady Rebecca, but I miss him still." She sighed softly, then gave herself a small shake. "But my son, the new Lord Hayward, has done very well in taking things on at the estate."

"I am glad to hear it," Rebecca replied, still feeling a trifle uncomfortable about the amount the lady was sharing when they had not been formally introduced. "I should go in search of my sisters now."

The lady's expression brightened. "But of course. Are you to have new gowns from Madame Bernadotte?"

Without meaning to, Rebecca allowed a heavy sigh to escape her, which, seeing the astonished look on Lady Hayward's face, only made a blush color her cheeks.

"Forgive me," she stammered, aware of her father's rumbling tones coming closer to her. "I did not mean to make any expression of complaint, Lady Hayward. It is only that, given that my mother is no longer with us, I have been given the responsibility of ensuring that my sisters and I are dressed appropriately. If I am truthful, I do not know precisely what would be best." She shrugged, heat still pouring into her face. "We have never been to London, and I do not know much about society." Quite why she was expressing this much to a lady she had never met before in her life, Rebecca could not explain, but there was something in the lady's expression that was so welcoming and encouraging that she felt as though she could tell her anything.

Lady Hayward tilted her head, her eyes considering. "I would be happy to assist you in this, Lady Rebecca," she said slowly. "I am aware that we have only just met, but if you have no other friends within London as yet to aid you, then I would be glad to offer my assistance."

"Assistance?"

Rebecca closed her eyes briefly, hearing the note of confusion in her father's voice.

"Father," she said quickly, turning to face the duke and seeing how his green eyes—so akin to her own—were watching Lady Hayward with something like suspicion. "This is Lady Hayward. She and I were quickly introduced as we came into this establishment. She is, very kindly, offering to do what she can to ensure that my sisters and I choose gowns of the highest fashion." Smiling quickly, she gestured to Lady Hayward. "Lady Hayward, forgive my improper manner. I should have introduced you properly." Praying that the lady did not think her entirely unsuitable for being anywhere near London, she tried again. "Might I present my father, the Duke of Landon."

Lady Hayward curtsied quickly, although she did not show any sign of awe or astonishment at being in the presence of a duke, as Rebecca had seen so many visitors do when they had come to the estate. "Good afternoon, Your Grace. I am very glad to meet you. As Lady Rebecca had just informed you, I would be glad to assist her with the ordering of suitable gowns for this Season." She smiled, and Rebecca saw the way the frown began to lift from her father's face. "In truth, it can be quite a burdensome task!"

Rebecca held her breath for a few moments, looking towards her father and entirely uncertain as to what his reaction might be. She prayed that he would be willing to permit Lady Hayward to do as she had offered for, whilst Rebecca had only just met the lady, she was certain that any assistance she could receive at this present juncture would be most appreciated.

The duke harrumphed for a moment, his gaze turning towards Rebecca, who continued to watch him hopefully.

"Very well," he said, speaking slowly as though he was not quite certain that such a thing was appropriate, his brow furrowing as he looked back towards Lady Hayward. "But only if it does not delay you, Lady Hayward."

Lady Hayward laughed and shook her head. "No, it does not," she replied with a smile. "In truth, I would be glad for the distraction! I have very little else to occupy me at present." Turning her head, she smiled at Rebecca, who, with relief, smiled back. "Might you introduce me to your sisters, Lady Rebecca? I should be glad to meet them."

"But of course," Rebecca said quickly, putting one hand on her father's arm. "Father, if you wish to wait, then might I suggest—"

"I would be glad to chaperone your daughters, Your Grace, if that would be of assistance."

Rebecca stared at Lady Hayward as she not only interrupted Rebecca but spoke with such a boldness that Rebecca herself was caught by surprise.

"As I have said, I have nothing else to occupy me at present and choosing gowns can take many hours," Lady Hayward continued, her eyes dancing as the duke's frown deepened at the obvious displeasure that came with knowing he would be forced to remain at Madame Bernadotte's for some time. "My carriage is only just outside, and I would be glad to return them to the house when we are finished here."

"How very good of you, Lady Hayward," the duke said, inclining his head just a little. "I confess that I am somewhat out of my depth when it comes to what my daughters require." His eyes studied the lady for a few seconds before he nodded. "It would be a great help to me if you would do as you have suggested, Lady Hayward. That would mean that I could continue with particular matters of business that require my attention." A slight narrowing of his eyes betrayed his flickering uncertainty. "But are you quite certain that you have nothing else to occupy you this afternoon? I should not like to take advantage."

Rebecca feared that Lady Hayward would take offense at this clear disbelief, for it was more than apparent that the Duke was not at all certain that Lady Hayward spoke the truth, but much to her relief, the lady in question did not appear at all perturbed.

"Your Grace, as I was telling your daughter only a few minutes before, my son, Lord Hayward, has purchased me a pair of gloves from Madame Bernadotte's, which I am now to collect. Thereafter, I have nothing at all to engage me for, like you, my son has matters of business to attend to."

"And you have no daughters?"

"I do," Lady Hayward replied, her expression gentling as she thought of the young lady, "but she is not yet out and remains at the estate. I am here in London with my eldest son in the hope of resolving a few matters of business. I will return home soon, of course, but not before such things are settled."

Hearing the two voices of her sisters echoing through the establishment, Rebecca turned a pleading gaze towards her father. "Might I take Lady Hayward to my sisters, Father?" she asked, but the Duke did not so much as glance at her. Rather, he fixed his gaze upon Lady Hayward, his eyes thoughtful as a look of interest drew into his expression.

"You are very kind to offer such a thing, Lady

Hayward," he said slowly, choosing each word with care. "I would be in your debt, should you be willing to bring my daughters home once their gowns have been ordered. However, I wonder if I might, thereafter, ask if you would be willing to speak with me at greater length once you have returned them to the house." He looked at the lady steadily, and a swirl of anxiety swept through Rebecca's frame. What was it her father was doing? And what was it he wanted? She could not imagine what he intended to say to Lady Hayward, and, from the way the smile was beginning to fade from Lady Hayward's expression, it seemed that she could not either.

"If you wish it, Your Grace," Lady Hayward replied, a line forming between her brows as she watched the Duke, seemingly intent on deriving his wishes a little better by studying him. "I will, of course, do as you ask."

The Duke smiled suddenly, a light coming into his eyes that had not been there before. It was as though Lady Hayward's agreement had brought a sense of delight to him, although still, Rebecca did not know what to make of it all.

"Excellent, excellent!" the duke exclaimed before turning back to Rebecca, one hand on her shoulder. "Now, Rebecca, you shall make certain that your sisters behave with all propriety. They must make an excellent impression here in London, even within the dressmaker's!"

"Yes, Father," Rebecca murmured, her gaze sliding towards Lady Hayward, who was, she noted, watching the Duke with interest. "I will, of course, do as you ask."

"Wonderful," the Duke replied, seemingly now very relieved that he would be freed of the burden of his daughters. "I shall return to the townhouse, then. Make certain to do all that Lady Hayward asks and listen to her advice." His hand lifted from her shoulder, but the familiar weight of responsibility immediately came. "And, of course, there is no need to concern yourself with the cost of such gowns, Rebecca. Choose whatever you wish and whatever is needed and have the bill sent directly."

"Yes, Father," Rebecca murmured, dropping her head as warmth entered her cheeks. She wished he would not speak of his wealth in such terms, not when Lady Hayward was present. It was, she considered, a little uncouth and ill-considered but, given that her father was not likely to listen to any word she had to say on the matter, Rebecca remained entirely silent.

"Capital!" the Duke boomed before bidding a quick farewell to both Rebecca and Lady Hayward and then making his way to the door. A tight band released itself slowly from Rebecca's chest as she heard the bell tinkle above the door of the shop, signaling that her father had left. A small sigh left her lips as she looked at Lady Hayward, who was watching her with a good deal of curiosity.

"I should introduce you to my sisters at once," Rebecca found herself saying, a little unnerved by the watchfulness in the lady's expression. "I—"

"You are often given responsibility for your sisters, I think," Lady Hayward said quietly. "Is that not so, Lady Rebecca?"

"It is, yes," Rebecca agreed, choosing not to hold back the truth from Lady Hayward. "My mother passed away when my youngest sister was only a babe. Since then, I have been given much of the responsibility of raising them and guiding them, although, of course, we have had governesses and the like." She tried to smile but found she could not, feeling as though she was unburdening her very soul for what would be the first time. "The three youngest are still at my father's estate, and, whilst I believe my father expects me to make a match this Season, I confess that I am not at all hopeful."

"Because you must seek out what is best for your sisters," Lady Hayward replied, clearly understanding everything Rebecca was saying without her having to express it directly. "Well, Lady Rebecca, mayhap that might change somewhat. Perhaps there is more I can do to aid you in this so that you have the opportunity yourself to find a suitable husband."

Rebecca's mouth lifted into a small, sad smile. "You are very kind, Lady Hayward," she said quietly, feeling as though she had known the lady for a good deal longer than only a few short minutes. "I will gladly welcome whatever it is you wish to offer."

Lady Haywood laughed softly, then gestured to someone or something over Rebecca's shoulder. "Perhaps we should start with the introduction of your sisters," she said as Rebecca turned around to see her sister, Lady Anna, standing only a short distance away, with something in her hands. "And then we must speak to Madame Bernadotte herself, to see what she requires of you all. No doubt, there will be measurements taken before we even consider what colors would best suit."

Rebecca felt the heavy burden of responsibility lift just a little as she turned around to lead Lady Hayward towards her sisters. This afternoon, at least, she would not be solely responsible for the gowns her sisters chose, the gowns that they would wear into society. She had Lady Hayward's experience and understanding now, even though they were only very briefly acquainted. For whatever reason, Rebecca felt as though she had found a caring and concerned individual whose eagerness to help came from a place of true kindness, and for that, she found herself increasingly grateful.

"Anna," she said, seeing her other sister standing a short distance away. "And Selina, might you join us for a moment?" Waiting until both had joined them, Rebecca turned to Lady Hayward. "Lady Hayward, might I present my two sisters." She gestured to the first. "This is Lady Anna, and next to her, Lady Selina."

Lady Hayward curtsied. "I am glad to make your acquaintance."

"And this is Lady Hayward," Rebecca told her sisters, who were both looking at her with a mixture of confusion and interest. "Father has returned to the townhouse and has left Lady Hayward to assist us in choosing our gowns. We will return with her once we are finished here."

Her sisters' eyes widened in evident surprise, but Anna was the first one to speak, excited tones pouring from her mouth as she engaged Lady Hayward in conversation almost at once. She spoke about colors and gloves and ribbons, begging Lady Hayward to join her so that she might show her what she had been considering. Rebecca smiled to herself, thinking that it was very much like Anna to be so eager, whilst Selina, as she expected, stayed back just a little, watching carefully but having none of the enthusiasm of her twin sister.

"You have only just met Lady Hayward, then?" Lady Selina asked as Rebecca nodded. "And Father is quite contented to allow her to help us?"

"*More* than willing, I should say," Rebecca replied with a sudden smile. "In fact, I do not think he was hesitant for barely a moment! The opportunity to return to the townhouse and to remove himself from supervising the choosing of gowns was one he could not simply ignore." She chuckled, and, finally, Lady Selina smiled. "I think we may have found an ally in Lady Hayward, Selina." A jolt of happiness ran through her frame, and Rebecca allowed herself to sigh with contentment. "Perhaps this Season will not be as difficult as I feared after all."

CHAPTER TWO

"I do hope there will be no tardiness this evening!"

Rebecca sat up straight in her chair as her father came striding into the room, only to stop dead as he caught sight of not one but three of his daughters sitting quietly together, waiting for him to join them. He cleared his throat and nodded at them, muttering something under his breath that Rebecca could not quite make out.

Rebecca felt delighted with his reaction, but, of course, hid it well. It would not do to have her father irritated just before they left the house for what would be their very first foray into society.

"Now that you have been presented," the Duke said, coming to stand in front of the small fire that burned in the grate, keeping the evening's chill away from the large room, "it is time to enter society. You are, however, to be on your guard."

Rebecca frowned. "If you are to suggest, Father, that we do not know what is expected of us in terms of behavior, then—"

"That is not at all what I am suggesting, Rebecca, and

kindly do not interrupt," the duke said firmly, his eyes fixing to hers as she quelled her frustration. "I am well aware that my daughters know what is proper and what is improper. I fully expect this evening to go very well, indeed. What I am to say, however, is that you all must be careful of those you are introduced to. Some will be eager for your acquaintance, of course, which will be rather flattering." His lips thinned, giving Rebecca the impression that he had been through an experience that had not pleased him. "It will be a matter of wisdom and consideration to know whether such people are eager for your acquaintance out of an eagerness to become known to you, or if they seek it out for their own gain."

Rebecca's heart began to grow heavy. She had been looking forward to this evening, especially with the promise of Lady Hayward being present also. The purchasing of their gowns had gone very well indeed and, whilst Rebecca did not know what Lady Hayward and her father had discussed thereafter, she felt quite certain that the duke would be very contented indeed with their acquaintance continuing. Now, however, she feared that her father would expect her to ensure that her sisters were acquainted only with those that were of excellent character and had no underlying motives—although quite how she was meant to decipher such a thing, Rebecca had very little idea.

"Therefore, you must be on your guard," the duke said firmly. "If, for any reason, a gentleman is eager to further his acquaintance with you, you shall give his name to me, and I shall do some investigation into his situation before any further interaction takes place."

"Yes, Father," the three young ladies murmured together, with Rebecca's heart sinking all the lower. She would never be able to find a suitable match, not when her father's demands were so stringent. What if she found someone she considered appropriate, only for her father to refuse on some small matter? She knew that the duke expected his daughters to marry well, to gentlemen of excellent title, of good family, and of substantial wealth. Now, it seemed, she had to find such a gentleman but would also be required to ensure that his character was without fault and his motivations quite pure. It felt like a near-impossible task.

The duke cleared his throat, his hands still clasped tightly behind his back, and Rebecca forced herself to give him her full attention and did not linger on any further thoughts at present.

"There is another matter that I wish to inform you of," the duke continued as Rebecca let out a long, slow breath, a little frustrated that there appeared to be even more the duke required of them. "It is to do with Lady Hayward."

Rebecca's heart dropped to the floor. No doubt, then, the duke had found something disparaging about the lady and had decided that she was not a suitable acquaintance for his daughters. Perhaps that was what had been discussed yesterday afternoon when they had returned from Madame Bernadotte's. Perhaps Lady Hayward had been thanked by the duke but asked to remove herself from their acquaintance. It was quite feasible, given all that the duke expected, and yet Rebecca felt sorrowful, having thought very highly of Lady Hayward.

"As you know, Lady Hayward is a kind and willing lady who has very little to occupy her at present," the duke began, his voice rolling through the room. "I was grateful to her for her assistance yesterday, and I am sure that, given how highly you all spoke of her, you were grateful for her company also."

"We were, Father," Lady Anna replied quietly. "I believe we all thought very highly of her."

"Good." The duke paused for a moment and, much to Rebecca's astonishment, began to smile. What was it he was going to reveal? She was no longer as certain as she had been about her father's intentions, praying that he would not ask them to separate from the lady entirely.

"Lady Hayward has a son. Three, in fact," the duke continued, now looking pleased with himself. "There are a few issues concerning the late Lord Hayward's will, and, in addition, I believe the new Lord Hayward is struggling just a little with all that has been placed upon his shoulders." He shrugged. "It is understandable when one takes the title to be a little overwhelmed, but there are certain matters that make things a good deal more difficult for Lord Hayward. Therefore, having discussed the matter at length with Lady Hayward, she and I have come to a mutually agreed arrangement."

A flurry of either fear or excitement—for Rebecca could not tell which—ran down her spine as she listened intently, wondering what it could be that had been agreed upon. It was not like her father to go about such things in this way, for he did not like to ask anyone for their help or assistance in anything, being quite determined to do it without interference. And yet, in this case, it appeared as though this was precisely what he had done.

"I have no interest in attending balls, in encouraging matches and in chaperoning waltzes and the like," the duke said with a wave of his hand and a sigh of exasperation. "Lady Hayward has no real interest in business matters, although, of course, she wishes to aid her son in any way she can. Therefore, we have both agreed to be of assistance to the other."

Silence filled the room for a few minutes as the three ladies looked at their father expectantly, clearly ready for him to say more, but it seemed as though the duke was finished with his explanations. With a shrug, he turned and gestured to the door. "Let us hurry now. She will be waiting."

Rebecca did not move from her chair. "What do you mean, Father?" she asked as Lady Anna and Lady Selina watched the duke with curiosity. "Lady Hayward is to assist you? In what way?"

"By chaperoning you, of course," he said, a slight flicker crossing his brow as though he had expected them all to understand what he meant without difficulty. "She will do what I do not wish to and will guide you through society and make certain that any gentlemen who wish to acquaint themselves a little more with you are entirely suitable."

WHAT A GIFT FOR LADY REBECCA! She now has the lovely Lady Hayward to assist her with her debut into the *ton* and help her find a husband. To find out what happens next, please check out **Mistaken for a Rake** on the Kindle store! Mistaken for a Rake

JOIN MY MAILING LIST

Sign up for my newsletter to stay up to date on new releases, contests, giveaways, freebies, and deals!

Free book with signup!

*Monthly Giveaways! Books and Amazon gift cards!
Join me on Facebook: https://www.facebook.com/rosepearsonauthor*

Website: www.RosePearsonAuthor.com

Follow me on Goodreads: Author Page

*You can also follow me on Bookbub!
Click on the picture below – see the Follow button?*

212 | JOIN MY MAILING LIST

Printed in Great Britain
by Amazon